THE
CRYSTAL
DROP

Also by Monica Hughes

THE
CRYSTAL
DROP

◆

MONICA HUGHES

SIMON & SCHUSTER BOOKS FOR YOUNG READERS
Published by Simon & Schuster
New York   London   Toronto   Sydney   Tokyo   Singapore

SIMON & SCHUSTER BOOKS FOR YOUNG READERS
Simon & Schuster Building, Rockefeller Center
1230 Avenue of the Americas, New York, New York 10020
Copyright © 1992 by Monica Hughes
First Simon & Schuster edition 1993
All rights reserved including the right of reproduction
in whole or in part in any form.
Originally published in Canada by HarperCollins Publishers Ltd.
SIMON & SCHUSTER BOOKS FOR YOUNG READERS
is a trademark of Simon & Schuster.
Designed by Vicki Kalajian.
Manufactured in the United States of America

10 9 8 7 6 5 4 3 2 1

Library of Congress Cataloging-in-Publication Data
Hughes, Monica. The crystal drop / by Monica Hughes.
p. cm. Summary: In the summer of 2011, the death of
their mother sends Megan and her younger brother
Ian on a dangerous journey across a Canada
ravaged by drought and the collapse of civilization.
[1. Science fiction. 2. Canada—Fiction.] I. Title.
PZ7.H87364Ct 1993 [Fic]—dc20 92-27706 CIP
ISBN: 0-671-79195-8

Thanks to Judy Hayman of Alberta Culture for introducing me to
the UNESCO World Heritage Site of Head-Smashed-In
Buffalo Jump near Fort Macleod, Alberta; to Dr. Grace Funk
for the story of "returning empties"; to Anne
Merriott for permission to quote from her poem
"The Wind Our Enemy"; and to the Alberta Foundation for
the Literary Arts for a Senior Writing Grant to assist me in
the research and writing of this book.

They said, "Sure it'll rain next year!"
When that was dry, "Well, next year anyway."
Then, "Next"
But still the metal hardness of the sky
Softened only in mockery...
Always hard yellow sun conquered the storm.
So the soon sickly-familiar saying grew
(Watching the futile clouds sneak down the north),
"Just empties going back!"

Anne Merriott
"The Wind Our Enemy"
from *The Circular Coast*, Mosaic Press

ONE

There was no sound now, and the room seemed emptier than Megan would have believed possible. She got stiffly to her feet. She pulled up the fold of sheet and spread it carefully up over the pillow so that it hid the still forms on the bed. Then it seemed somehow disrespectful to turn away from the silence, and she backed slowly out of the bedroom into the kitchen, shutting the door quietly behind her.

But she hadn't been able to shut the silence inside the bedroom. It seeped out into the kitchen and filled the room, pressing against her eardrums. She became aware of the thudding of her heart, of her breath being pushed in and out of her lungs, of her heart squeezing, relaxing, pushing the blood to her lungs, around her body. She spread her hands out in front of her, brown freckled hands, the palms callused, the nails broken and bitten. When she held them up to the brilliant light streaming through the window, she could see, faintly, the outline of bones beneath the skin and flesh.

Death. It was the most final thing there was. No turning back from it. Like the buffalo in the old days, thundering across the prairie, coming to the cliff, not being able to stop, falling down . . . down . . . down. She doubled her hands into fists and shivered in spite of the stifling air in the kitchen. What was supposed to happen now? What was she supposed to do? There was no one to ask. No one to turn to for help. *She* was in charge.

Her eyes wandered around the familiar room, looking for an answer. The old range and refrigerator stood against the south wall, unused since the electric lines blew down the year after Ian was born. Mom had always cooked on the small wood stove against the west wall. In winter the chimney pipe, running through the two bedrooms, took the edge off the cold.

On the south wall, above the useless electric stove, hung a calendar with a photograph of Lundbreck Falls on it. It came from Mitchell's Hardware in Lethbridge and the date was 1998. The edges of the paper were yellow and curled, but the torrent of sparkling water still cascaded over the rock face into a river that never ran dry. Above the falls was an island green with bushes. The calendar had hung over the stove for as long as Megan could remember. Lundbreck Falls, up in the foothills past Pincher Creek and Cowley. Where Uncle Greg had gone, Mom said.

Mom. Her hands clenched convulsively and she turned away. The sun reflected off the side of a tin can among the litter on the porch outside and was caught in the crystal drop that hung by a nylon thread in the southeast window of the kitchen. A thousand tiny rainbows moved lazily around the room as the crystal turned. A fat bluebottle fly suddenly wakened and buzzed angrily against the widowsill beneath the crystal drop. It was an enormous sound, like a buzz saw starting up, and Megan jumped. She thought of the implications of the growing heat. Of the bluebottle . . .

She squared her shoulders and pushed open the screen door to the porch, unthinkingly letting it bang behind her, shattering the silence. She felt her hand go out to still the door, heard herself calling out "Sorry, Mom" as she had done a thousand times before.

Tears blurred her vision as she hunted for a spade among the clutter of broken chairs, old crates, and useless tools. It was gritty with rust, festooned with cobwebs. She brushed it off and walked down the steps with it in her hand.

Once she was beyond the shadow of the porch, the heat struck her. It was like the flat of an angry man's hand across her face. She cringed from it and almost turned back, away from her unwanted task. Then she straightened her shoulders and stared out across the prairie, her eyes half-shut against the glare.

Ahead of her, due east, the land stretched away to a hazy horizon, cut only by the ruler-straight road that ran past the farm to the distant highway. South of the farm there had once been a lake, silvery with water. Was that her memory? Or was it one of Mom's stories about the past? As she stared, leaning on the spade, an image of blue sky reflected in a fold of land slowly surfaced in her mind.

There was no water now. Not in the lake. Nor in the irrigation canal west of the farm. The grasshoppers clicked and rustled, leaping against her legs, falling to the hard ground, leaping again. Their unending clatter filled her head with noise, so that it was hard to think straight. In the wire enclosure four Plymouth Rock hens scrattled in the dust for seeds and greenery. They had just about eaten the patch bare. Their squabbling voices blended with the higher notes of the grasshoppers. It was the sound of heat. Of heat and drought.

Megan walked slowly northward, away from the house but not too far away, looking for a patch of ground that was a little less cracked, a little less stony than the rest. She came to Mom's old vegetable garden, nothing growing there now but a patch of pigweed. She pulled it up and stuffed it in her skirt pocket. Greens for the chickens and some for dinner, with whatever Ian and Charlie had managed to find, she thought.

As she jabbed the spade down into the earth, the shock jarred up her thin arms and into her chest. She placed her foot on the flat shoulder of the blade and put all her weight on it, heaving the spade to and fro to get some purchase. Now she was able to drive it into the ground perhaps an inch, with a scattering of pebbles and dust. She moved the spade and tried again, looking for a more yielding spot. The sun beat painfully against the back of her cotton shirt. Her callused hands burned and the sole of her foot, in its thin canvas shoe, ached from the spade's edge. She gritted her teeth and stabbed again.

In an hour she had scraped an area about three by five feet, but nowhere more than two inches deep. Below that the ground was rock hard. She looked down at all she had managed to accomplish and collapsed to her knees. Now, for the first time, the tears ran salty and hot down her cheeks, splashing on the ground, making dark circles of moisture that spread, then faded and vanished as the thirsty sun sucked the moisture back up into the dry sky.

"I can't do it alone. I can't!"

She forced herself upright again, leaning on the spade, and looked around her. There were Ian and Charlie. Two small moving dots against the yellow dust and silvery sage. Her face felt stiff with drying tears and she rubbed her hands roughly over her cheeks. Then she put two fingers in her mouth and whistled. The two dots stopped, changed direction, came closer, were lost in a dip in the ground, and appeared moments later on a ridge of sand.

"I got four gophers, Megan." The boy was shouting almost before he was within earshot. "One for each of us and one for Charlie. He really helped a lot."

He arrived panting, the dog bounding ahead, and stared at Megan's spade and the shape of the plot she had been trying to dig. "What's going on? What are you . . . ?" He looked up at her face and his own paled, the freckles standing out on his skin.

Megan put an awkward hand on his bony shoulder, drawing him close to her. His body was like the stove, radiating heat against her front.

"Mom's dead, Ian. And the baby too." Dry, necessary words.

"*Mom?* She can't be. What happened? It was just a

baby being born, wasn't it? Just a little baby." His fists beat at her chest.

"I don't know nothing about birthing. Just the animals, a long time ago. It was so easy then. It wasn't like that with Mom. I did everything she told me . . . " Her voice broke, but she forced it steady for Ian's sake and went on. "It just wasn't any good. And when the baby finally came it was real scrawny-looking and kind of blue. He . . . " She stopped and swallowed.

"He? You mean I got me a brother at last and he's gone and died. Oh, *shit!*" He pulled away from Megan's encircling arm and kicked at the pebbles.

"Ian Dougal, don't you ever let me catch you talking like that or I'll wash your mouth out with soap!"

"You ain't my mom." The words were out of his mouth before their meaning became real. His lip trembled. "Oh, Megan, what're we going to do?" The tears made runnels in the dirt of his cheeks.

"Hush, Ian. It'll be all right. I'll look after you." Her arm tightened around him again and for an instant he let himself be hugged against her bony chest. Then he pulled away.

"You're not my mom. You're just my sister."

"That's right. And you're my brother. And we're all each of us has got, so we'd better stick together, okay?"

"Guess so." Reluctant, he scuffed the dirt with his shoe.

"First off we've got to bury Mom and the baby before the day gets real hot. But I can't. I've been trying for hours." She stabbed at the caked earth with the rusty spade.

"That ain't never going to work."

"Try it, Ian. Just for a bit. My hands are smarting from that darn spade."

"Now who's swearing?"

"*Darn* doesn't count, you know that. Here, you try."

Ian stabbed half-heartedly at the ground. "We'll never get through this, Megan. Only way's to soften it."

"How, for pete's sake?"

"Water, of course."

"That's the craziest idea I've ever heard, Ian Dougal. We're pumping less from the well every day. Ain't no way we can waste water to dig a grave."

"You don't have to scream at me then. Come on, Charlie, let's go."

"No. Please. I'm sorry. It's just . . . Oh, Ian, I don't know what to do!"

Ian turned back. "Megan . . . I don't know. But there's the irrigation canal. It's half full of sand already. Would it do all right for . . . a grave? It's easy digging."

◆

It was almost sunset by the time they had buried Mom and the baby in the wind-driven sand and covered the grave with stones that lined the edges of the canal, "in case of coyotes." Ian had crossed his arms on his bony chest and shivered when Megan had said that. She hammered together a simple cross from two slats out of an old kitchen chair and took a stub of pencil from her skirt pocket. She began to print in slow wobbly capitals:

ROSEMARY DOUGAL

BORN MARCH 21, 1973

"How d'you know that?"

"Got it out of the front of the old Bible. I wonder what's the date today."

"I dunno. It's about 2020, isn't it?"

"Course not, silly. Not nearly. Mom was about thirty-eight. Seventy-three and thirty-eight is . . ." She counted on her fingers and then began to write again.

DIED SUMMER 2011

BABY . . .

"What'll we call the baby, Ian?"

"Let's call him Charlie."

"You can't call a baby after a *dog*, stupid. I dunno. I guess I'll give him Dad's name. That's what Mom would've done, I bet." She pressed the words into the wood with the pencil stub:

BABY DON, BORN AND DIED, SUMMER 2011

They planted the cross deep in the sand, propped around with stones, and walked slowly back to the house. Behind them the sky flamed scarlet and gold, but they hardly noticed it. Sunsets were always that way these days. It was the constant dust in the sky, Mom had said.

Indoors the emptiness of the house shouted silently at them. "I'll light the fire if you skin out your gophers." Megan busily broke up pieces of an old crate, one of the last. What'll we do when there's no wood left? she wondered and began to talk loudly to banish the silence and her own scary thoughts.

"I'll stew the pigweed, and we'll roast the gophers over the fire. Two each. They're thinner than they used to be, Ian. And tougher. Hey, don't give the best bits to Charlie. You need feeding up worse than him."

"They're my gophers."

Megan sighed. "I guess you'd better have my second one, but it's got to be for you, mind. Not for Charlie. Give them here. The fire's hot enough now."

As they ate, the house grew dark. There was no lamp oil and no candles left. The dying glimmer from the stove only made blacker the shadows that lurked in the corners of the room. Ian shucked off his shoes and overalls and crawled into the truckle bed in the small bedroom they shared. Charlie lumbered across the worn floor and flopped down on his feet. Within a minute they were both asleep.

Megan prowled through the empty house. She ran her fingers over the slick surface of the calendar, imagining the coolness of the waterfall beneath her fingers. She touched the crystal hanging in the window. Then she slipped outside, being careful not to let the screen bang.

The eastern sky was dark, laden with stars, the land beneath it empty and silent, as dark as the sky. She could remember, years ago, when there were farms out there, yard lights like fallen stars, and in the distance, like the Milky Way, the lights of Fort Macleod.

She walked all around the outside of the house. In the faint afterglow of sunset she could see the low line of the Porcupine Hills. Somewhere beyond them were the Rockies. Somewhere over there in the west was the waterfall. Water. Flowing endlessly.

She climbed the porch steps and settled in the old rocker, her feet tucked under her. She tried not to let herself think of Mom and the new baby over in the irrigation canal. A distant coyote howled its loneliness to the sky and she shivered and wrapped her arms around her thin chest.

She rocked and tried to concentrate on the facts. She and Ian were alone. The water that dribbled from the pump grew more alkaline each day. When Ian got hot and gulped too much of it, he got the runs. The gophers they had had for supper were lean and stringy. The patch of pigweed was one of the last.

Was Father ever coming home? Should they walk east to Lethbridge and try to find him? Suppose he wasn't there? Suppose he'd gone to Calgary? More likely Edmonton, where conditions weren't so bad, folks had said, long ago, when there were neighbors to talk to. He could be anywhere. Or nowhere. Maybe he was dead. Like Mom.

The coyote wailed again and its howl was like the pain inside Megan's chest. She hunched her knees and dropped her head and let the tears she had held back since she had dug the grave run down her cheeks. She didn't cry for long. Her body was too dry for the luxury of many tears. She crouched silently in the old rocker until at last she fell asleep.

She woke, stiff and cramped, with a blood-red sunrise in her eyes. As she went to the outhouse she looked automatically to the west for clouds, but there were none. On the way back she noticed that one of the hens had died. It was less of a tragedy than it would have been a month or so before. The hens had given up laying and were fit for nothing but the pot. She picked it up, shaking away the ants that had already arrived, and sat on the porch steps to pluck it.

It was a horrible job without boiling water to loosen the feathers, but they could afford neither the water nor the fuel. Anyway it was too hot to light the stove. As she pulled out the black and gray barred feathers, she made up her mind what had to be done, and when Ian stumbled out of the house, his pinky-fair hair standing on end like a rooster's comb, she told him what she had decided.

"We're leaving."

"What d'you mean? Where'll we go?"

"West." Megan's voice was confident. To the east lay five hundred miles of drought and grasshoppers. "We'll head west toward the mountains and find Uncle Greg." And the waterfall, she said in her heart, but not aloud. Ian didn't understand how she'd always felt about the waterfall.

"Mom's brother Greg lives up beyond Lundbreck. I remember her telling me. That's why she kept the calendar. I'm going to go through her stuff and see if I can find his letters—he used to write, back when there was a mail service. I bet Mom kept his letters."

"But suppose Dad comes home and we're not here?"

Megan sighed. "He's not coming back or he would have already. We've just been kidding ourselves waiting. He left when Mom told him about the new baby coming. I could see in his eyes then that he wasn't a-going to come back."

"What did you see, smartie?"

"Fear." Megan folded her lips tightly, pushing down her own fear.

"You look like Mom when you do that," Ian said, his voice wobbling.

Megan wanted to hold him in her arms and ruffle his hair and tell him it was all right, that she'd take care of him. But she couldn't. She'd only enough courage for herself, with nothing over for sharing.

"Get dressed," she said and walked into the house swinging the plucked chicken by its neck.

She dropped it on the cutting board and opened the cupboards one by one. There were dishes, unmatched and cracked. There were glasses from a long-gone gas station. There were about four cups of flour left in the tin canister, and there was a jar half full of home-made coffee made of parched grain and dandelion roots. That was all. The berries they'd picked and dried last fall were all eaten. The canned goods they'd bought in Fort Macleod before the last store closed were only a memory, the emptied cans rusting in the garbage pit behind the house.

"There's nothing to stay for." She was convincing herself as much as Ian. "The water's giving out. We'll die if we stay here. You do see that, don't you, Ian?"

"I suppose." The words came out slowly, and she saw the pale flash in his eyes that she'd seen in Dad's seven months before, when he'd taken the horse and left.

"It'll be okay, you'll see. I've got a plan. We'll spend tomorrow trapping all the gophers we can. We'll skin them and dry the meat. We can pick fresh greens as we go, and once we get to the mountains there'll be berries. It's so hot it must be close to berry-time, don't you think?"

She grew more confident as she talked. Talking made it seem almost real, as if it had already happened. "We'll each take a jacket and all the food we can get together, in a blanket roll. And containers of water, as much as we can carry. I think we can walk ten, maybe twelve miles a day, don't you? It won't take us that long to get to the mountains."

Ian stared at her and didn't say anything for a minute. Then, "If it's such a great idea, how come Mom and Dad didn't leave? How come we're still here?"

Megan hesitated. "I dunno, Ian, honestly. Maybe Mom didn't want to travel with the baby coming . . ."

"But why not *before*? Why not years ago when I was little and everyone else left? Why're we all alone out here?"

She shook her head. It ached and her eyes felt hot and swollen. "I dunno," she said again. "But I'm sure Mom'd want us to go now. Certain sure. We can't live on gophers and barley kernels forever."

"But *Dad*. Suppose he—"

"I'll leave a note for him under the jug on the kitchen table. I'll tell him we're going west to Lundbreck. When we get there I'll leave another message somewhere, maybe at the post office, if there's still a post office there."

"How d'you know about things like writing and post offices and where other places are? How do I know you're not just making it all up? Maybe it's just stories."

"It's *not* stories, honest, Ian. Don't you remember, when you were little, before Fort Macleod closed down? I got to go to school then, on a bus the color of egg yolks. It'd stop at the bottom of the lane, and I'd run down with my lunch pail and you'd wave me good-bye. Don't you remember? And I learned to read and write and figure, and lots about the world. Till they closed the town in second grade and the bus never came no more." She sighed. "Then Mom taught me, till she got too tired. But I read all her books. Adventures and stories about the real world too."

She cut off the chicken's neck and expertly gutted it. She spared a teacupful of water to wash it and her hands, and she tossed the guts out into the yard for Charlie and the ants and any passing crows.

"So go look for gophers. All you can get."

"But I'm hungry."

"There'll be stewed chicken and dumplings when you

get back, okay? And take your hat. Hasn't Mom told you a thousand times—" She stopped too late.

Ian looked at her as if she'd just hit him, grabbed his cotton hat, and jammed it on his head. "C'mon, Charlie."

"I'm sorry. I didn't mean—" The screen door slammed.

Slowly she pumped water into the battered pot and dropped in the chicken with a spoonful of salt. She broke up one of the last crates on the porch and lit the stove.

Once it was going well she got a basket and trowel and went out into the grasshopper-noisy heat. About a half mile south of the house was a patch of what had once been marsh land close to the old lake. The last time she'd been here, there had still been a few small patches of green. There were fewer this time.

She picked leaves and dug as many roots as she could grub out of the dry dirt: goat's beard, plaintain, and dandelion. When her basket was full she trudged back through the grasshoppers that rose in noisy clouds around her knees. We can eat them too, she thought, if we have to. Roasted. On our journey. And we can trap ground squirrels maybe, up among the rocks. She added matches and a pot with a lid to her mental list of things to take.

Ian came home later, long enough later for her to

begin to worry, with a clutch of gophers in his hand. His face was pale and glistening and he said he felt sick, so she made him lie down with a damp cloth on his head while she skinned out the gophers, cut the meager flesh into thin strips, and climbed the outside ladder to lay the meat on the roof. The shingles were hot enough to bake bread, she thought. In a few hours the meat would be bone dry and hard. So long as the hawks didn't spot it first. She squinted up at the molten sky, her hand shading her eyes. It was empty.

She crawled down the ladder, dizzy with heat, and into the ovenlike shade of the house. Ian was asleep, his face damp and clammy, blotched white and pink. I bet he took off his hat once he was out of sight, she thought. Charlie raised his head and thumped his tail once, but didn't move from his favorite place on Ian's feet.

Megan went into her mother's room, smoothed the bedclothes, and lay down. This room, in the northwest corner of the house, was the coolest. Any breeze coming from the mountains came first through this window. There was no breeze today. No clouds either. Sometimes clouds came out of the west, but they only drifted past, small white packages of . . . nothing.

When the sun showed in the corner of the window she got up and went through the drawers of the chest. I'm sorry, Mom, she said to herself. I don't mean to pry, but I need to know. There was nothing of note in the drawers. Underwear, washed and mended. Two sweaters. Mom's brush and comb. A cardboard box that had once held shoes. In it was an old watch, which Megan shook and wound up. The hands remained unmoving at twenty-three minutes to four. She put it back. There was a faded snapshot of Dad, its edges woolly with holding. Under that was a small packet of letters.

"Sorry, Mom," she whispered again, and opened them, one by one. They were all quite short, a single sheet, and they were all from Uncle Greg. The most recent was dated June 23, 2005. More than six years ago. The year Fort Macleod closed down and the school bus stopped coming, Megan remembered. It was then that the telephone and electricity stopped too.

She scanned the letters, stray phrases jumping off the pages and sticking in her head. ". . . west of Lundbreck, not far from the falls." "We call our new community Gaia, after the Greek name for Earth. We aim not just to survive, but to help Gaia heal herself." "Things are going to get worse, Rosemary. If you and Don want to bring the children . . ." "Our sixth year. Thirty of us now. A good crop, despite minimal rainfall. I think we'll make it." That was the last letter in the package. Megan folded them carefully, put them back in the box, and closed the drawer.

She left Mom's room and went to check the chicken. It smelt mouth-wateringly good after days of gopher stew. She tossed in the green leaves she had dug and mixed flour and water with chopped chicken fat for dumplings to cook on top of the stew.

"I don't want to get up. My head hurts," Ian grumbled when she woke him for supper.

"You'll feel better when you've eaten, honest. It's the heat. And not having breakfast."

His color was better when he'd finished the chicken stew and dumplings, and he offered to take Charlie gopher-hunting again.

Left to herself, Megan began to pump water to fill the water bottles she planned for them to take. They were old round metal canteens covered with cloth, with tight screw tops and carrying straps. Dad had picked them up at an army surplus years and years ago. They smelt a bit musty and she had to waste almost a cup of water rinsing them out. She had only filled the first when the water began to turn muddy. I'll leave it to settle again, she thought, and finish filling them in the morning. She remembered Mom saying that one of the reasons they'd liked this farm was the never-failing spring of sweet water close to the house. Never-failing. Till now.

She picked the rest of the meat off the chicken bones. Enough for soup. They'd have it tonight. It would be good to go to sleep on a full stomach. Since there was still a fire in the stove, she made the rest of the flour into a paste with water and baked flat-cakes on top of the stove. Hard and dry, they'd be good journey-food.

The sun dropped behind the Porcupine Hills and the long twilight began. Ian and Charlie should be back soon. She climbed onto the roof. From there she could see them far to the east. She waved and the small figure waved back. She gathered up the dried meat and took it back inside, wrapping it in a cloth.

"No more gophers," Ian said. "Well, we caught three, but Charlie just gulped them down before I could stop him. I'm sorry, Megan."

"It doesn't matter. Poor Charlie didn't get much of our chicken, did he? I guess he's entitled to gophers. I've got chicken soup for supper. Isn't that grand? *Two* meals today."

They scraped up every last drop, knowing that in this heat no food could be kept for more than a few hours without spoiling. By the time Ian had finished, his head was nodding onto the table.

"Come on. Bed. It'll be a long day tomorrow."

"Are we really going to go?"

"Yes, really. Bright and early, before sun-up. While it's still cool."

"Megan, I'm scared. What if—?"

"Going's safer than staying, honest. Lundbreck's only

about thirty, forty miles away. Three, four days' walking. Easy. Come on. Get your shoes and overalls off.
Into bed."

"What'll be there?"

"Uncle Greg for a start. People living in big houses
maybe, with water coming out of the taps. And shops
where you can buy bread and milk and eggs and green
stuff."

"How d'you know all this?"

"Mom told me. She told me lots of stories, especially
last winter, with Dad gone. She said that every spring
the snow used to melt into rivers all pouring down
from the mountains, and the irrigation canals would fill
with sweet water. The farmers used to pump it out and
spray their fields. Imagine, great sprays of water moving
to and fro across the land, turning it all green behind
them. Green just as far as you could see."

His eyes closed and she stroked his hair. It was harsh,
sun-dried, and spiky under her hand. Inside her was a
sweet pain, like nothing she had ever felt before. It
made her feel weak, soft. She took her hand away and
got quickly to her feet. She mustn't allow herself to be
tender with Ian, to be motherly. She had to be strong
for both of them, as hard as the land. Not soft.

Back in the kitchen she planned and packed. In the
morning she would fill the second water bottle. The
three remaining hens she'd take alive in a basket, either

for their own food, or as trade for a night's lodging and fresh water. She wrapped the flat-bread and dried meat and roots and tied the bundle securely. A pot with a lid. A good knife. Matches. A change of shirt, socks, and underpants, that was all. Ian had only one pair of jeans that weren't falling apart, and they had patches over their patches, hand-me-downs from the days when they'd been hers. And she had just the skirt she was wearing, made by Mom from a checkered cotton table-cloth. When they got to Uncle Greg's, she promised herself, they'd have decent clothes again. She put in jackets, in case it got cold in the hills, and a blanket each to roll it all in, with a piece of rope to hold it tight and carry it. With the water bottles and the hens, that would probably be all they could handle.

She looked anxiously at the bundles. Had she forgotten anything important? Would Ian be able to carry his load? *Was* she doing the right thing?

Be strong, she told herself. Be hard. She went back into her mother's room and lay on the familiar bed and stared at the cracked ceiling until at last she fell asleep.

TWO

They had walked more than half a mile due west along the dirt road, and had just crossed the sand-filled irrigation canal where they'd buried Mom and the baby, when Megan stopped short.

"Ian, where's your sun hat?"

He muttered something and Megan, already tired after a restless night and hot with her burden of bedroll, cooking pot, and the basket of hens, lost her temper. She grabbed him by his thin shoulders and shook him till his teeth rattled. "Where is it?"

"Guess it's back at the house. Megan, you're hurting!"

"You *know* what Mom said. There's a hole in the sky and the bad light comes through and gives you cancer. How can you be so stupid? I *told* you."

"I forgot." He was blubbering now, his upper lip shiny with mucus.

"You'll just have to go back for it."

"I won't. I'm too tired. You're just an old meany, Megan. And I don't have to do what you say, anyway. You're not my—" He stopped, stricken, and looked back at the bridge across the canal.

The hardness in Megan melted. "I'm sorry. I'm sorry. I keep forgetting you're just a little kid." She looked around. The ground was flat, sand and sage. The only shelter from the sun was under the bridge. "Climb down the bank and crawl under. Take the hens with you. They'll die in this heat." She passed him the basket. "I'll go back for your dumb hat."

She dropped her load to the ground with a groan. All the way home and out again! Over a mile wasted and already the sun was up, heating the land. She walked as fast as she could, walking off her anger.

Back at the house the kitchen already looked abandoned, as if it knew they'd gone for good. The note to Dad lay under the purple jug that had always stood in the middle of the table, with all the knives, forks, and spoons in it. She found Ian's hat at last on the floor of the bedroom and scooped it up impatiently.

As she crossed the kitchen on her way out, the calendar above the electric stove caught her eye, the water frozen forever falling. "Soon," she whispered. "We're coming." The crystal drop turned in the window, burning gold in the early sun. Like fire and water both. Magic. Good luck, maybe. Impulsively she pulled it free. The nylon thread was long enough to make a loop, and she hung it around her neck, the sun-warmed crystal below her collar bone.

Ian's hat in her hand, she shut the front door and let the screen bang shut. With its noise echoing in her head she walked back to the canal. There was smoke in the sky over in the northwest. A grassfire. Coming this way.

She stopped on the bridge and called her brother's name. "Ian!"

At first there was no sound but, as she listened, she became aware of a strange hollow booming. It seemed to come from the west, from the Porcupine Hills. An unreal sound, like ghost voices, like the hills themselves talking to her. Warning her! She shivered.

"Ian!" she yelled again, and he came scrambling up from under the bridge. "Did you hear that?"

"What?"

"I dunno. A spooky kind of noise." She shivered.

"There's an old owl under the bridge, roosting," Ian told her, and Megan laughed, the sudden terror falling from her like a snake's old skin.

"Come on, silly billy. Let's go." She handed him his hat.

"Where're we going, Megan? I mean really. D'you know? Have you got a map?"

"It's in my head. The main highway's down south. That way. It follows the river up into the mountains. That's where we're going. We won't follow the highway, though. We'll take the back roads, the trails. It'll be all right," she finished confidently. Confidently enough to quiet Ian's fears, though not her own.

They walked on silently. At first Charlie raced ahead and chased imaginary gophers, but soon he began to pant and paced himself to Ian's small strides. About an hour's walk from the farm they came on the dirt road going south and turned down it without argument.

There was no shade anywhere. The road was edged with barbed-wire fences, the posts so worn and rotted that the wire seemed to hold up the posts instead of the other way around. One steer pushing against it and it would all come tumbling down, thought Megan, but of course there were no steers anymore. Yellow sand, silver-gray sage. A sky relentlessly blue and, on their right, the flat-topped silhouette of the Porcupine Hills. Ahead of them, pinky in the heat-haze, the low line of the Rockies.

"See those white bits shining?" Megan pointed. "That's snow."

"Megan, I'm so tired. And thirsty."

"Just a little bit farther," she pleaded with him. This is only the first day, she thought. The first hours. And already he wants to give up. How'll I ever get him across the hills and up to Lundbreck?

"Look, there's an old shed down there. It's not far."

The shed was roofless, little more than a couple of walls, but they huddled in its shade until the worst of the afternoon heat had passed. Megan's throat was dry and her lips cracked, and Ian whined for water, but Megan hardened her resolve and rationed the water sternly.

She peered into the basket. The three hens lay limply, their beaks opening and shutting convulsively. She wetted a sage leaf and trickled water, drop by drop, down their throats.

"You care more about them darn hens than me," Ian complained.

"You're not going to drop dead this moment for lack of water," she retorted. "As long as the chooks are alive they're like money. They'll pay for water and a bed for the night. Without them we've got nothing to offer."

A hawk circled suddenly overhead, its shadow racing across the sandy field toward them. The hens cringed away from the shadow and Megan covered their basket with her spare shirt. Then she lay back among the sage and slept.

It wasn't until late afternoon that she woke, groggy and disoriented, with Charlie panting in her face. She rolled away from his doggy breath and stumbled to her feet. We've wasted half the day, she thought anxiously. We've got to get to the hills before nightfall.

"Come on, Ian, wake up." She shook his arm and straightened up to stare westward. Only a couple of hours' walking. That's all it'll take to get to the hills. Then we'll have to work southward around their base and head west. Into the unknown . . . with nothing but a vague memory and the picture of a waterfall in her head. How long would their journey take? She didn't know. Would they really find food and water? She didn't know.

Am I crazy? Am I leading Ian and me to death?

Death in the hills. Or death back on the farm.

Overhead the hawk slowly circled a thermal. "Get out of here," she screamed at it. "Go away. We're not dead yet!"

Ian scrambled up beside her, blinking sleepily. "What's all the yelling about? Who were you talking to?"

"Nothing. Nobody. Come on. Let's pick up our stuff and get moving. We've slept far too long. I want us to be *there* before sunset."

When she pointed to the base of the hills, Ian groaned. "We'll never make it."

"Of course we will. Come on." Megan picked up her roll and the basket of hens and set off briskly. Before long a track turned right, running west toward the hills. The track, too, was fenced and lined with the ghostly skeletons of tumbleweed. A black tatter waving from the barbed wire ahead made her heart lurch for a moment. Was it a dead crow, caught in the wire? Or some other dead thing? But it was just a shred of black plastic, part of the old days. She'd seen the stuff before, blowing by, catching on fences and bushes, an indestructible bit of the past.

The cart track ran, straight as a ruler, toward the hills. As they drew closer Megan could see that there were actually three main hills, formed of a series of steplike layers of rock, each riser showing the bare rock through, like rows of grinning teeth. Directly to their left the hills sloped gently downward to the south, and only one ridge of rock grinned at them.

"Look, Megan, the trail stops."

She pulled her eyes from the hills and stared. Ian was right. The trail ended at an abandoned farm, little left but weathered silvery wood. Tufts of sage and speargrass covered the gently rolling land beneath the Porcupine Hills. To her left was a thin line of darker green.

"There's a creek over there. Maybe there's still water in it. Come on."

It was tougher going on the rough ground. Sage roots seemed to reach out and grab their tired feet. Speargrass drove its barbed seeds into their ankles. Underfoot the grasshoppers rose and, as they neared the base of the hills and the greenness of the creekbed, ground squirrels dashed across in front of them.

Charlie whined deep in his throat and gave chase.

"Call him back, Ian. If he heads off we'll never get him back."

"Charlie! Come back here. Charlieee!"

Reluctantly the dog came back and submitted to being patted and having his ears pulled.

"I've got a bit of string in my pocket. Maybe…"

"No *way* he's going to be tied up. Charlie, you'll mind me, won't you, there's a good boy? He'll stay close, Megan, honest."

Megan smiled reluctantly at the sight of them: Ian—small, scrawny, freckled, with hair pinky-blond and tousled under his sun hat; Charlie—an overgrown lump of rough brown fur, thick-muzzled, but with an astonishing silk plume of a tail, a dog of no known lineage, but deeply, slobberingly affectionate, and with an incurable appetite for gophers and ground squirrels.

The fold of green land had no visible water running through it. Underground seepage from the rocks above must be enough to keep the saskatoon bushes green and laden with fruit. They ate all that were ripe and Megan filled the pot with half-ripe berries. "They'll cook up with our gopher meat. Or one of the hens."

Now they were close enough to the lower slope of the hill to see a faint trail wandering upward, hairpinning to and fro. It had once been a foot trail, Megan guessed, though now it was almost overgrown with the encroaching sage. "But it'll take us up to the top. It's up there. Much easier walking."

"But where'll we stop for the night?"

"We'll sleep out. You'll love it, Ian. You'll see the stars all around you. Like magic."

There was no more talking once they reached the path because its steepness took all the breath they had, with none left for words. As they climbed higher Charlie grew more and more restless, growling deep in his throat. Suddenly, taking them both by surprise, he leapt up the hill, not following the path, but going straight up, his claws scrambling on sand and rock. He vanished from their view.

"Charlie! He's gone. Charlie. Where are you? Charlie, come here!"

"Stupid dog!"

"He answered me. Didn't you hear?"

"I didn't hear a thing. It was an echo, I expect. Just your own voice, Ian."

"It wasn't any old echo. And I saw something move. Up there. On top." He pointed.

"Where? Why, that's not Charlie. It's half his size and kind of chubby. And look at its tail. Nothing like."

They had come to a place where the trail stopped climbing and turned left to run parallel with the top of the bluff. Above them were maybe twenty yards of cliff face. Obstinately Ian set his feet to the rock.

"You can't go up there. You'll fall and be killed."

"I don't care. I'm gonna get Charlie back. He's all I've got now."

It hurt surprisingly, like a knife straight into her stomach. Megan blinked and swallowed. "You've got *me*, Ian. Isn't that enough?"

"You're my sister. I *need* Charlie. He's my *friend*."

She dragged him back from the cliff, blubbering and punching her with his small fists. "Stop it, Ian! Hush up and listen." She shook him. "Look there. Farther along the path. D'you see where the cliff's sort of broken down? There's a slope. We can climb up there."

They hurried along the overgrown path and scrambled up the broken scree to the top. It was almost completely flat, like a gigantic tabletop. For an instant the splendor of the view took Megan's breath away and she forgot about Charlie, about Ian and the worry of making decisions. When she looked back she could see the way they'd come all spread out like a map. To the northeast was the dark scar that had once been Mud Lake. To the north, out of sight behind the far hill, must be their farm. Directly in front of her, to the east, the land stretched to the haze of the horizon, sandy-gray except where it was cut by a thin line of green, snaking away from northeast to southwest and out of sight behind the curve of the hill. The valley of the Oldman River, like a pale ghost of what it must once have been.

"Charlie, where are you? *Charliee*!"

She spun around, almost losing her balance at the cliff edge, in time to see Ian running at full tilt along the cliff top to her right, his bedroll abandoned on the stony ground.

"Wait for me!" She hid both their bedrolls and the basket of chickens under a leafless bush and ran after him.

Ahead of her was a metal railing that must have once been painted white. It enclosed a circular area that overhung the steepest part of the cliff and led back, via a concrete path, to . . . "A house? It can't be!"

She ducked under the fence onto the concrete path, which snaked southward along the top of the bluff. A small breeze, not enough to cool the sweat on her face, stirred the hot air. She gave a half-hearted yell after the dumb dog and ran along the path. Where was Ian now?

The path stopped outside the building, the strangest she'd ever seen. It was sunk into the ground and made of slabs of material the same color as the sandstone hills upon which she stood. On the flat roof grew straggly sage and speargrass. To its right, anchored to the hillside, stood a windmill, made of a strange silvery metal with vanes set in a drum-shape at the top of its mast.

She was alone. There was no sound but the insistent clatter of grasshoppers and the swishing of the mill.

"Ian! Ian, where are you?"

She stood frozen. Her heart felt as if it were made of stone. First Charlie vanishes. And now Ian . . .

"Megan, come on!"

The air rushed into her lungs in a thankful gasp and she ran forward, yelling furiously into the empty air. "Where are you hiding? Come out, you stupid idiot, or I'll skin you alive!"

"Here. Inside."

There were double glass doors. Megan pushed them and they swung open, letting her in. "Ian, come away. You don't know—"

"Look, Megan, there are stairs. It goes down and down." He clattered recklessly down and she had to follow him.

"Inside the hill?" she wondered out loud, and then thought, no, down its side, down the cliff. A cliff-house, one floor piled on top of another. But even though she tingled with curiosity at the thought of a house built into a cliff and why they hadn't seen it from below as they approached the Porcupine Hills, a part of her mind warned: *Watch out. Be careful.*

Ian had vanished down a second flight of stairs, and Megan followed him, passing another room below, dimly lit by skylights in the ceiling above. Yet another flight of carpeted stairs led directly down to an even stranger room. In its center was a frame made of great posts lashed together, as if for the framework of a gigantic tipi, and within were grouped a collection of enormous stones, each too heavy for a single person to have lifted. And who would carry huge stones into a house? Megan wondered. In the back corner of this strange room stood a real small tipi, the kind Megan remembered from the long-ago days when she was little.

As eagerly as Ian, she ran down the next flight, noticing, as she ran, that each room was like a balcony overlooking the floor below, each lit by skylights in the ceiling of the previous level. At the next level, in the place where the end wall in an ordinary room would be, were three huge bulky shadows. Beyond them the floor stopped. There was only a deep well-like space filled with darkness. "Ian, stop!" she cried as he ran heedlessly forward. She followed reluctantly, suddenly afraid of the sheer bulk and stillness of the shadowy

shapes; but before she could reach him several dark figures rushed at them from out of the shadows. Megan
felt her arms twisted behind her back. A blindfold covered her eyes.

"It is forbidden to see," a strange voice whispered in
her ears. She was pushed forward, blindly stumbling
down a sloping passage and down yet another flight of
stairs. A hand was hard on her shoulders and she was
forced to her knees.

THREE

Megan stumbled, falling forward onto hands and knees, feeling the rough greasiness of ancient carpet and the smell of dust. The blindfold was suddenly snatched from her eyes. She blinked and stared. In the dim, echoing space a single shaft of light fell on a cliff face directly in front of her. She looked up. And up. Into the faces of three huge hunchbacked and hairy beasts. They were going to fall—to leap—from the cliff top directly onto her.

Automatically her arms went up above her head in futile protection against the danger from above, and she crouched back on her haunches. From all around, echoing in the vast space, came the sound of mocking laughter. Faintly, through the crazy laughter, she could hear Ian's frightened wail.

The thought that he was in danger shook Megan out of nightmare into reality. She yelled, "Don't you dare touch him!" She peered through the shadows and realized that the huge space was just another room, that the cliff wasn't real but made of plastic. Above her, the sunset colors filtered redly through dusty skylights upon . . .

"Why, they're just a bunch of stuffed animals!" she exclaimed.

An unseen hand struck the side of her head, not hard enough to mean serious damage but enough to sting.

"Watch your tongue, woman. Buffalo spirit in those bodies."

"Yeah. Strong spirit. Stronger than you. So watch out." Another voice echoed the first.

"This Napi's world. The buffalo Napi's gift to the people. What you doing in Napi's world, white woman?" Was that a third voice? They seemed to come mysteriously from behind her, from around, blurred and distorted by the echoes.

Megan, still kneeling on the floor, tried to turn and identify her tormentors, but as soon as she moved two strong hands came from behind, grasping her shoulders, forcing her down. She tried to wriggle free and felt a foot between her shoulder blades, pushing her against the floor so that her lips and nose were pressed against the grimy dust.

"What are you going to do? What do you want with us?" Megan's voice was muffled and wobbly. The pressure of the foot against her back increased.

"We ask you that first. Answer! What you want in Napi's world?"

"Nothing. I'm sorry. We didn't mean . . . we were just looking for Charlie."

"Charlie? Man? Or boy?" The voice was hard, suspicious.

"N-neither. Charlie's my brother's dog. He ran off up the cliff, so we had to come looking. We thought maybe he'd come in here. What *is* this place?"

"Like I say, Napi's world."

"Who's Napi then? Are *you* Napi? One of you?"

Megan felt a stillness among the invisible figures, as if the whole room had reacted to her words. Her heart thumped, wondering what she had said wrong. Then the awful silence was broken by laughter, not the mocking scary laughter of before, but belly laughter, rolling around the space, echoing up past light and shadow.

In spite of her fear and bewilderment she felt the corners of her own mouth tug and widen in response to the laughter. The foot was removed from her back and she was pulled roughly to her feet.

"Ian, are you okay?" She peered around, dazed by the contrast between the dark room and the light coming in through the skylights above.

"Megan!" He came running at her, butting his head against her ribs, his arms tight around her waist. Her arms went around him and she could feel his heart pounding through his thin ribs. The need to protect him made her feel strong and equal to anything.

"How dare you scare my kid brother, you . . ." She glared at their tormentors, four of them, young men not much older than herself. They were dressed in jeans and loose shirts, and three of them wore their straight black hair tied back in ponytails, while the fourth wore his loose to his shoulders, under a beaded headband. They were lean and wiry, high-cheekboned, with black eyes that flashed with mischief but gave nothing away. When they moved forward under the light of the skylights, the shadowiness of their skin barely lightened to a warm brown.

"Why, you're natives, aren't you?"

"We Peigan men. Napi's people."

There was that strange word again. *Napi*.

Long-ago memories sifted up through Megan's consciousness as she stared at the strangers. Memories of the times before. Visitors on Sunday afternoons. Lemonade on the porch and Mother introducing her to someone.

She bobbed a curtsy. "How d'you do? My name is Megan Dougal and this here's my brother Ian. We've got . . . that is, we used to have a poultry farm on the road just north of Mud Lake."

The four looked at each other, nudging, jostling each other, teeth flashing white in their shadowy faces. They giggled, suddenly no longer terrifying figures from nightmare but unsure youths.

It was the one with the beaded headband who broke the silence. "I'm Mike Spotted Eagle. Dick Yellow Calf over there. Wally Running Rabbit. And this here's Tim Fast Rider."

"How d'you do?" Megan repeated. Ian's grasp around her waist relaxed and he peered shyly out at the strangers. "He's not used . . ." She tried to explain. "He's seen no folks other than his ma and me for a long while."

"She around?" It was a casually asked question, but Megan became aware of a sudden stillness, a kind of interior waiting, as if her answer might affect mightily what they would do next.

"She's dead." She spoke drily, her chin up, her eyes looking straight into the almost-black eyes of the leader. His eyes were flat, giving nothing away. "She died birthing our little brother. And he died too. So we left the farm."

"Where you heading?"

"West. To a place called Lundbreck Falls. Do you know it? About fifty miles away, I guess."

"Miles? White-man talk! How many days' walking?"

"We won't know till we've got there, will we?" She tried to outstare him, saw his mouth twitch. She grinned and he grinned back. Out of the corner of her eye she saw the other three figures relax. She thrust her hands into the pockets of her skirt so he couldn't see her hands trembling. "D'you live here? In this place?"

Ian broke away from her, ran forward, and peered up the cliff at the stuffed buffalo. "It's weird. Really weird."

"Hush up," hissed Megan. But it was all right. Mike was smiling.

"Like I say. We Napi's people. This here's Napi's world."

"But who is Napi?"

The four looked at each other.

"Old Man."

"Trickster."

"Made us."

"Gave us the buffalo."

Out of this confusion Megan seized on the one that made a kind of sense. "But there aren't any buffalo. There haven't been any buffalo for ages and ages."

"That's right." Mike wasn't smiling anymore. He

grabbed her wrist and pulled her across the room. To the left of the artificial cliff was a wall and on the wall a long tablet. "Can you read?"

"Of course I can. I went to school for two years. And then Mom taught me lots of stuff. And we had books—"

"Read what it says here, then." He jabbed at the plaque with his thumb.

Stumbling over the long words Megan began:

" 'One hundred twenty years ago was the last use of the Head-Smashed-In Buffalo Jump'—but that's not very long ago after all."

"This was wrote when they built the place. Back in 1981. Go on."

"So it's really a hundred and . . ." Megan counted on her fingers. "A hundred and fifty years ago. 'Five hundred years ago Columbus discovered America. Nine hundred years ago Norse sailors landed in Newfoundland. Two thousand years ago was the birth of Christ. Forty-five hundred years ago Stonehenge was constructed.' What's a 'stonehenge'?" she interrupted herself.

"Dunno. Go on. The next bit's important."

"Sorry. 'Five thousand years ago the Great Pyramid was built. Fifty-five hundred years ago was the first known use of the Head-Smashed-In Buffalo Jump.'"

"That's enough. Did she say it okay, Wally?"

Wally nodded silently.

"Wally can read," Mike went on. "But I have the stories in here." He put his hand on his chest. "Makes me leader. Right, Wally?"

"Right, Mike."

"Right, guys?"

The others nodded.

"But I don't understand." Megan stared up at the plaque.

"No more buffalo. Right? Like you said. More than fifty-five hundred *years*. Napi's gift to the people. Then nothing. No more."

"Was it the drought? Our chickens—"

"More like a flood than a drought." Mike's face was dark.

"Show her, Mike," said Dick Yellow Calf.

"And the kid." Tim Fast Rider pushed Ian forward. "Show them, eh?"

"Not now. Getting too dark."

"I know the words by heart, Mike." Wally, the reader, wanted to show off, Megan could tell.

"She got to *see*, ain't she? Got to *know*. Tomorrow we tell them about Napi and the buffalo. And about *her* people."

"That's very interesting, Mike. But we really ought to get going. It's a long way to Lundbreck."

"Stupid to travel at night. Catch your foot in a gopher hole, right? Can't go far with broken ankle."

"Can't find water. You need water to travel."

"But . . ." Megan was feeling increasingly uncomfortable. It wasn't anything she could put into words. Just a sense that these four were like a . . . a gang, maybe, with plans of their own that had nothing to do with her need to get to Lundbreck.

"Got good meat for supper. You welcome to stay and share."

"Well . . ."

"Yeah, we got lucky, didn't we, guys?"

"Guess you brought us luck, eh?"

They batted the words to and fro, like a ball in a game. A lot more was going on than Megan could understand, but there was not much she could do about it.

"Thank you. We'd be glad of a meal and a place to sleep," she said guardedly. I won't tell them about the hens, she thought. Not till morning. They'd probably take all three. I don't trust them. Not yet.

And when Ian piped up with "We've got—" she knew what he was going to say and pinched the back of his hand to silence him, hoping the men wouldn't see.

But I hope the hens are safe in their basket, she thought worriedly. If a coyote should smell them, it'd never let a basket stop it.

It was by now almost entirely dark in this strange high room, only a faint gray light seeping through the skylights of the upper levels. At a word from Mike, Dick and Wally went up a flight of stairs opposite the mock cliff and vanished into the shadows.

Megan looked around and saw that to her left on this lowest floor there was another faint source of light. Another way out, she thought. Ian tugged at her sleeve and whispered urgently. She could see glass blocks in an outer wall. A heavy swing door. She walked quickly toward it and had her hand on the pull before the man called Tim caught up with her.

"Where are you going, girl?"

"Just to the outhouse. This is a way out, isn't it? Ian and I need to go."

Tim laughed. "Hey, Mike, she wants the outhouse."

"No outhouse here. We class people. We got an *in*-house."

As Megan turned from the swing door she saw that she would not have been able to leave even if Tim had not stopped her. A heavy bar had been slipped through both sets of door pulls.

"Don't like surprise visitors," Tim volunteered when he saw her staring. He held out a candle in a rusty tin-can holder. "Here." He pushed open another door. The walls inside were of pale tile with a sifting of dust over them, but when Megan rubbed her finger on the wall she could see how they must once have shone. It was smelly in the small room, but no worse than the outhouse back home, which hadn't been redug since the summer before Dad left home.

"We throw a pail of water down once a day. Keeps it clean. *And* you can wash up." He turned on a faucet. Water gushed out.

Water. Clean water coming out of faucets. She tasted it. Cool and sweet. She put her face near the spout and gulped.

When she and Ian were through, she asked Mike about the water.

"Good spring underneath. Windmill on top pumps it up. You see windmill? There's other rooms with toilets and faucets, but they got blocked up. This only one working now."

Megan wondered what the four would do when the last toilet ceased to work. Dig a hole outside for an outhouse like everyone else, she guessed. When she held the candle high she could see pale plastic panels in the ceiling and guessed that behind them had once been electric lights, like they'd had at the farm before the lines blew down and weren't repaired because everyone in Fort Macleod had left.

"Food ready soon," Mike said. "Come."

She and Ian followed him and Tim up a broad flight of stairs and along a curious open-sided passage like a long porch that overhung the floor beneath, wrapping it around on three sides. Wally came out of another room, an oil lamp glimmering in one hand. His shadow leapt darkly as he moved toward them. The light flashed on something white in the corner. Something gruesome. Megan stared and flinched away. A pile of skulls!

"Buffalo. *Dead* buffalo." Mike was staring at her. Though his lips were smiling, his eyes were flat and dark, not smiling at all. He seemed about to say something else, but then he changed his mind. "Let's see if that meat's ready to eat."

He led them into a room warm and steamy, smelling of fried meat, gravy, and herbs. In it were perfectly ordinary small white metal tables and chairs, the first real furniture Megan had seen in this peculiar house.

Against the far wall was an electric range, like the one at home, only three times the size. Mom's hadn't worked since second grade. This was obviously working.

"Wherever d'you get the electricity?" This seemed to Megan more magical than any of the crazy things she'd seen today, perhaps because it was understandable. A stove was a stove, but electricity had to come from somewhere else, made by mysterious people who sent it through the wires.

"Sun God."

Mike's voice was dead serious and, when Dick snickered, he slapped him across the face.

"You didn't have to do that, Mike." Dick rubbed his cheek. Then he turned to Megan. "Did you see those platelike things up top? Where you came in. They suck the sun's heat into batteries and when we want the stove we turn a switch and the heat comes on."

"Sun God," said Mike obstinately. "You remember that, Dick."

"Okay. Okay. But don't you forget it was me fixed the little wires made it work again, man!"

For a moment Megan was afraid that they might start fighting, but then Wally distracted them by bringing a big iron skillet from the stove and putting it in the middle of the table.

They picked the strips of meat from the pan and ate it with their fingers, dipping it in the gravy. Nobody talked. Megan ate until she felt the skin across her stomach stretch and tighten.

Across the table Ian's head nodded forward, jerked back, and nodded again. She pushed his plate out of the way before his hair fell in the gravy. "It's been a long day." The words came naturally, without her having to think them out. Mom's words in the old days, when she wanted to get folks moving.

"There's a big room across there where we sleep. Carpet. Padded seats. Cosy and dark."

"Ian and I stay together." She outstared Mike's impudent eyes.

He shrugged. "Suit yourself, woman. There's the tipi. You can sleep there, if you want."

She remembered it, two floors up from the place where they now ate, and nodded. "Come on, Ian." She hauled him to his feet and helped him stagger sleepily upstairs. It was almost totally dark now. Just a glimmer of moon through the skylights.

As they climbed the dusty stairs, she tried to forget the menacing presence of the three great buffalo over to the right there. Only stuffed animals, she told herself. But now, in the moonlight, they seemed to be more than just stuffed animals, as if the Trickster, Napi, had given them a spirit life of their own. She swallowed a sudden panic, turned her back resolutely, and with an arm around the sleepy Ian, climbed up to the room with the boulders on the floor and the tipi in the corner.

Its enfolding presence was comforting in the strange vastness of this place. Ian curled up on the floor and was instantly asleep. Megan lay beside him, her arm over his shoulders. The hard floor seemed to tip and sway beneath her.

How tired I am. What a day it's been. Have I done the right thing? she asked herself over and over again. Mom, what should I have done? She fingered the crystal at her throat.

Her ears were full of the moan of the owl beneath the bridge, of the clatter of grasshoppers, the chittering of ground squirrels, and the scream of the hawk. And other, closer whispers. Were they the ghosts of this place? Or only the mischief of Mike and his friends?

Just before Megan shot down a dark chute into sleep, her memory played back the last sound she'd heard before they had climbed the cliff and found this strange place. The bark of a dog. *Charlie*! I forgot all about him. Where can he have got to? Well, nothing I can do now, but first thing in the morning I'll have to look for him again.

◆

She woke early to find herself staring at a square of light on the floor outside the tipi. Where was she? Then all the memories of yesterday and the day before came flooding back. Mother and the baby. Blood. Stillness. The grave in the irrigation canal. For a moment she felt she just couldn't bear it. She had to get out. To run like crazy, letting the wind blow away the bad memories.

She crawled past Ian without waking him and walked quietly up the remaining flights of stairs to the top floor of the cliff house. It grew steadily lighter as she climbed, and the top room was flooded with the redness of early morning.

The doors through which she and Ian had come so easily yesterday were now bolted and barred, as the other doors had been, with a rod pushed through the handles. No one could get in, through top or bottom of this strange cliff house. Why had it been left open yesterday? she wondered. And who, in this empty land, were the four men trying to keep out with their locks and bars?

She leaned as close to the windows as she could. The sun had just risen and she could see, to the extreme left, the dark line of Mud Lake between the sparse grass below and the pink smudge of the horizon. Another baking day.

She became aware of a faint click-click sound, puzzlingly regular, unlike the ragged chorus of the grasshoppers, and realized after a time that it was the sound of the windmill vanes spinning in the strong wind, pumping up fresh water from the depths of the earth. For how long would the spring below the cliff house run? Everything else was dry or alkaline. Whoever built this place must have dug the well very deep. But then, money must have been no consideration because the house was as big as a palace. But in spite of its depth, even this spring would probably run dry one day, as everything else had, in the kind of reverse magic that had changed good prairie dirt into sand, lakes into sloughs, and sloughs into dry gullies.

She went slowly downstairs again, looking at the pictures on the walls. There was a horse, reminding her of old Sally, who'd carried Dad to wherever he had gone last winter, never to return.

There was a big horned animal called an elk. Pronghorns. And over and over, like the chorus to a song, pictures of the buffalo.

" 'Napi is the mythic creator of the Blackfoot people,' " she read. Well, why couldn't Mike have said so, instead of all that strange talk about Old Man and Trickster. She wandered around, looking at prairie grass and rocks. There were written explanations of everything, but she didn't understand a lot of the long words, so she gave up and went downstairs again, to the floor with the great smooth stones enclosed in a circle, the floor with the tipi in the corner in which Ian still slept, untroubled by the worries that crowded Megan's head.

She sat on the central boulder in the middle of the circle and felt oddly soothed and comforted. By whom and why had this odd building been made? "Napi is the mythic creator of the Blackfoot people," she said again out loud. Like a god, she thought. Perhaps this place is a church. It is certainly more like a church than a house. Napi and the buffalo. And the people. Peigan, Mike had said. They were part of the Blackfoot, weren't they? And they had a reserve south of the Old-man River.

When she heard voices below she got to her feet and leaned over the guard rail in time to see them come from their sleeping place. Yawning, scratching, they didn't seem as scary as they had last night among the shadows. They were talking together, but the echoes distorted their voices so she couldn't make out the words. They looked up, saw her, and Mike jabbed Tim in the ribs. They stopped talking then. Dick and Wally went off to the kitchen and Mike looked up at Megan. The light falling on his upturned face showed the high cheekbones, the jutting nose. His head looked as if it had been carved out of a beautiful piece of dark smooth wood.

"You stay there. I show you Napi's world before we eat."

"I already looked around up there," she told him after he'd climbed the stairs to stand beside her.

"What you see?"

"What it used to be like before the rain stopped. Grasses. Pictures of animals. Stuffed ones too. There's a marmot—like the one we saw back there on the cliff. I think that's what set Charlie off, chasing the marmot. It looked like a big dog itself."

"Charlie?"

"Ian's dog. I told you, remember? He ran off. Probably far away by now." She sighed. "Poor Ian. It'll break his heart."

"Gone. Like the buffalo. And the deer." His voice was accusing, almost as if it were her fault. "Once there were stories written on those stones." He pointed to the circle where she had been sitting.

"On the *stones*?"

"A kind of magic made of light, Tim said. Tim's uncle worked here long ago, in the old days."

"Worked here?"

"Yeah, showing visitors the buffalo jump. Talking about the old days. Like a museum. Thousands of white folk come, from all over the world, Tim's uncle said. I asked him once, 'Were they sorry about the buffalo and the people?'"

"Sorry? Didn't it just happen, like the drought and the hole in the sky?"

Mike shook his head vigorously. "Napi's world not like that. Sure, some good years, some bad. Grass fires. But behind the grass new growth and then more buffalo and deer. Plenty meat and hide. Berries and roots enough for the people and nothing Napi gave us ever wasted. Come. I show you."

He led her down a single flight of stairs, to show her cases containing bowls, cutting knives, and scraping tools, pictures of all the uses of the buffalo. And he described the hunt.

"The men drawing them in from all across the Porcupine Hills, one man in a calf's skin leading them on, crying like a calf so the lead cow'd follow. The others planting sticks and brush along the sides, getting narrower and narrower, so the buffalo had to get closer and closer together. See." He showed her a contour map in a glass case, brushing the dust away with the side of his hand. "Hundreds of buffalo, from right across the top of the Porcupine Hills. Took days leading them in, gentle, like Napi, not stampeding them. They'd come close between the lines of brush, all moving forward. And then they couldn't stop . . ."

Mike had her by the arms now, was pushing her forward until she was against the edge of the mock cliff, looking down the sheer drop to the floor two stories below. She tried to relax, not to let him feel the terror stiffening her body. He was, she was beginning to suspect, just a little crazy.

"How many years our people hunt the buffalo over this jump? Remember?" He gave her a little push.

"O-over fifty-five hundred years."

"And then?"

"They went away, didn't they? Like the rains, like the winter snow, like the new grass in the spring. They just went away. Last night Wally said it was like a flood, but that's crazy, isn't it? A flood on the prairies!"

Mike pulled her back from the edge and led her silently down another flight of stairs. "Here's your flood." He let go of her wrist and gestured at the wall. What was it? Megan blinked and saw blurred pictures, enlargements of ancient photographs of bearded white men, of trains, men with guns shooting into a stamped-ing herd of buffalo from a moving train. And, in the farther corner of the passageway, the silent accusing witness she had glimpsed the night before—the pile of whitened buffalo skulls

"But it all happened so long ago. More'n a hundred years."

"The buffalo just the beginning. Right? Then the rest. Tearing up the land for wheat so nothing'd hold it down when the wind come. Draining the good swamp for more land. Moving rivers. Damming them. Chemi-cals poisoning air and earth and water. Poisoning Napi's good world. Yeah, white man's driven Napi out of his world. Now see what's left. Nothing."

She pulled away and faced him. Once, long ago, Dad had faced an angry bull with nothing but a switch in his hand. Hitting the bull over its nose, making it back off. "So what are *you* doing about it?"

For a moment her attack took him by surprise. Then he laughed shortly. "Me? I'm gonna make Napi's world again. Pray him back with sweetgrass. Like in the old days. Away from the others down there on the reserve, the Oldman River nothing but a trickle, the land blow-ing away. Me and my friends, we stay up here away from all that."

Megan hoped briefly that Napi was not the sort who

liked human sacrifices. Somehow she didn't think so. Nothing she'd seen here gave that impression. But Mike *was* crazy.

She swallowed her fear and spoke out. "I've just buried my mom and the new baby. Ground too hard to dig, we had to put them in the irrigation canal where the sand's all blown in. So I know what you mean about the land. But it was none of *my* doing nor my mom's. Now we're going upriver to Lundbreck, like I told you. There's a place . . ." She hesitated. Wanting to share her dream of water falling over a cliff, on and on, the spray making rainbows, not knowing how. "Ian and me, we're going to settle there. With our uncle. Make things work and grow. Maybe bring Napi back—*our* way."

She stood in front of the pile of buffalo skulls, out-staring Mike. He looked gravely back at her, and she had no idea in all the world what might be going on behind those flat black eyes. The spell was broken by Ian's voice.

"Megan, where are you? Megan, I'm *starving*!"

Wally came out of the kitchen. "Grub's hot."

"We can't take any more of your food," Megan began stiffly. "But we'd be grateful for a drink of—"

"But, Megan!" Ian ran down the stairs.

"There's plenty." Mike's voice was gruff and he

looked oddly ashamed, not as tall and all-powerful as he had a few minutes ago. As if the magic had run out of him.

What had caused the change? Megan wondered. "Well, if you're sure . . ." she began reluctantly.

"Plenty for all, eh, Mike?" Wally grinned. "Since we got lucky."

Mike frowned and Wally's grin faded. "I'll go put it out." He turned away.

They ate silently in the dim kitchen, Ian tucking into huge slices of fried meat. Is he underfed? Megan wondered anxiously. He was certainly small, though wiry. Was he normal for a ten-year-old? She really had no one to compare him to. She herself still felt satisfied from the huge meal she had eaten last night and ate only a single piece of fried meat.

When he was through eating, Ian bounced up and began to explore the room, opening drawers and cupboards until Mike roared a "No!" that brought him up short, his mouth open. It had been a while since a man had shouted at Ian.

"Ian, where's your manners?" Another of Mom's expressions slipping out.

Ian knew it. His lip stuck out obstinately. She tried coaxing. "There's lots of interesting things to see out there. Pictures. You don't have to know the words. Go on now."

"I want to go look for Charlie."

"Not now. We'll look later, Ian, I promise. Don't worry. He's probably hunting gophers somewhere nearby."

He left the kitchen reluctantly and Megan turned to the others. "We should be on our way. Thank you for—"

"Got to show you the jump first. Before you go."

"But I've seen it already." Megan's eyes went to the artificial cliff, the cluster of stuffed buffalo at the top.

"No. Not that one. The real one. Outside."

Megan's heart jumped. She hadn't been entirely sure that they would let her and Ian go without a struggle. And with the doors locked . . .

◆

Ian wandered around the rooms as Megan had told him, staring at the stuffed animals, the displays of dried grass and old bowls. Boring stuff. He kicked at the edge of a case and looked cautiously around. Bossy old Megan had vanished upstairs with the big man with the beaded headband, and the others weren't in sight. Maybe he could sneak into the kitchen and get some more of that meat. Hide it under his shirt maybe. Better than those darn gophers.

He opened the door slowly and peered around the edge of it. All clear. The kitchen was empty, the tin plates stacked in the sink. Against the far wall the white refrigerator gleamed invitingly. He ran across the room and swung the door open.

◆

Megan followed Mike upstairs to the door through which they had come the previous evening. Mike lifted out the heavy metal bar, unfastened the bolts, and opened the door. The hot smell of parched grass and sage flowed in.

The sun glared white on the concrete pathway. Megan could feel her pupils contract, her eyes water, her skin sting and tighten. The heat was like a blow from a flatiron.

"Come." Mike led the way along the path that snaked along the top of the cliff. At its end, where she and Ian had crawled through the railings in search of Charlie, the path widened into a kind of circular platform, a waist-high railing protecting them from the drop below. Looking down, Megan could see clearly the trail they had followed the day before. It wrapped itself around the curve of the hill and zigzagged upward.

Directly below the railing, at the extreme north end of the lookout, the ground fell abruptly into an eroded gully about thirty feet down. In the long-ago time before the cliff had fallen, the distance to the bottom must have been over sixty feet. On the far side of the fallen area the rocky overhang sheltered a colony of cliff swallows, their mud nests glued to the underside of the overhang like small overturned pots.

"Read," Mike commanded, pointing to another plaque, this one fastened to a great boulder at the end of the lookout.

The writing was smeared with bird droppings, the letters encrusted with blown sand. Slowly, with several false starts, Megan managed to decipher the message.

"'Here the dramatic hunt came to an end. If all went as planned, stampeding buffalo plunged over the cliff, bodies piled up around. Most died in the fall. Others were killed by hunters standing by.'"

Megan tried to imagine a huge herd of buffalo stampeding toward the edge of the cliff, unable to see the certain death that lay ahead of them. Why hadn't they stopped or turned before it was too late?

As she looked across the barren land that stretched away to the eastern horizon, the sun gave her the answer, shining blindingly in her eyes. The buffalo were doomed as soon as their hooves were set on this eastward path.

She imagined what it must have been like. The noise of thundering hooves, dust rising in clouds. The screams as they fell. The animal smell and the thick sweet stench of blood rising from the gully below.

In spite of the heat she suddenly shivered.

"You can see better over here." Mike's voice was soft in her ear.

She allowed him to help her over the railing. His hand under her arm, she let him lead her toward the rocky overhang beyond the eroded portion of the gully. She found herself moving forward, as in a dream, toward the light. And Mike's voice murmuring in her ear.

"All those years. How many years?"

"Fifty-five hundred."

"And then nothing. Our life gone. Taken away. The land measured out in squares. Cut up. Drained. Used. Look out there. See what the white man's done to Napi's land."

The brightness swam in front of her eyes. She could see nothing, feel nothing, except the hand under her arm urging her forward. Toward the light . . .

Ian's scream shattered her trance. She teetered for a second on the very edge, turned from the light into a world suddenly blood red, spinning with green circles of sun behind her eyes.

Ian was running along the path toward her, howling, blubbering. She tore herself away from Mike's grasp and stumbled toward him. They met at the railing and he hurtled through it, flinging himself against her stomach.

"What is it? What's happened?"

"Charlie. Charlie." He choked, tears and mucus running down his face.

"Where? What's happened?" And, looking up, seeing the expression on Mike's face, she knew, even before Ian blurted out the tearful words.

"*Dead.* I saw his skin. And the meat in the fridge. It was Charlie. They made us eat *Charlie*!"

FOUR

Megan felt her stomach heave. Mike's eyes were on her—black, flat, giving nothing away. No way I'll throw up in front of him, she told herself. Over Ian's head she glared at the others, Wally and Tim with mocking smiles, Dick looking kind of scared. Had he been the one who had actually caught and butchered Charlie? Poor dumb Charlie, who thought the whole world was his friend and only lived for the joy of Ian's love and the hunting of gophers.

Ian's howls turned to shuddering gasps. She could feel him stiffen against her. In a minute *he'll* throw up, she thought, and that'll be as bad. She pulled back and slapped his face, not hard, just enough to sting.

"Don't you dare," she snapped. "That's about the best meal you've had in six months and the best you'll get till we hit Lundbreck, so just you hang on to it. Ain't nothing's going to bring Charlie back now, so stop that!"

It wasn't really her talking. She'd have never said anything that spunky. It was more like Mom. Mom's iron courage and common sense. Ian stopped his spasmodic shuddering in mid gasp and stared at her, his mouth open.

"Come on, Ian. We're leaving." Megan prayed that her anger would stay hot enough to make her legs work, to get them away from this place, out of sight of the four men, before her memory had time to replay what had happened just before, on the edge of the buffalo jump.

She grabbed Ian's hand and turned, heading up the gentle slope, westward, away from the jump, away from Napi's world and the four men standing there. She wouldn't look over her shoulder to see if they made any move to follow them, but she walked so fast that Ian had to trot to keep up with her. The ground was hard, stone and sand, with small scrubby patches of sagebrush. The only thing they had to watch out for was not to catch a foot in a ground squirrel's hole.

As soon as they were over the top of the hill, close by a dried-up slough that offered a sparse cover of wolf willow, Megan released Ian and crouched in the shade of the brush. "Get down," she panted and rolled on her stomach to look back the way they had come, her heart pounding against the hard ground.

The gentle curve of the crest of the Porcupine Hills cut the brilliant sky from north to south. Nothing moved. She waited, trying to breathe evenly, quietly. A sudden shadow on the ground made her flinch. She looked up. Just that old hawk again, following them around. She wished it would go away. If Mike should see it hovering above them—and how could he miss it, the only moving thing in this empty land?—he would know exactly where they were.

Little by little her ragged breathing quieted and her heart stopped its wild thumping. She peered again through the concealing branches of the wolf willow. Nothing out there but a single ground squirrel, sitting bolt upright like a tent peg, staring at them. Unafraid. It wouldn't be there if Charlie were nearby, Megan caught herself thinking.

Ian had got his breath and began to snivel again.

"It's okay." She tried to put her arm around his shoulders, but he batted it away.

"I hate you, Megan Dougal. You hit me."

"I'm sorry, Ian, honest. I had to do it. You'd have got

all high-sterical if I hadn't. We had to get away from *them*."

His voice wobbled in the silence that followed. "What'll we do now?"

Megan tried to push her own unexamined fear out of her mind. Later, perhaps, she would look at it. She tried to make her voice sound confident, as if she knew what she was talking about.

"We'll wait a bit longer, just to make sure they're not following us. Then we'll circle back from the north to the place where I left the bedrolls and stuff. Once we've got them back we'll head west, over thataway, till we hit a road. There's bound to be a road." I wish I had a real map, she thought. Not just a dream of a waterfall and a vague direction. Go west.

"Suppose they catch us?"

"They won't. We'll be real careful."

The sun swung overhead. The air shimmered and the grasshopper song was like a shimmer too. The hawk had gone and the sky was as empty as the land. Even in the shade of the sparsely leafed brush it was baking hot.

"They'll have gone indoors now, away from the heat. Come on."

Megan led the way up the small slope away from the creek. When she stood cautiously upright she could see the white railing and the windmill gleaming white over to her right. Directly ahead of them, behind that rocky outcrop, was the place where she'd left their bedrolls.

"You stay here, Ian," she whispered. "Flat on your tummy. If . . . if they should catch me or anything, you run. Okay?"

"Where to, Megan? Where'll I go?"

Megan thought about it and took a deep breath. "Listen, Ian. If anything happens to me, now or maybe later on, you're to go west till you hit a track going south. If you go south you'll hit the Crowsnest Trail sooner or later. That's the main highway. There'll still be traffic, I bet. You're going to have to stop a car and ask the people to look after you. Got it?"

"Me? Stop a *car*?" Ian's eyes were round. He'd never even seen a car close up, Megan remembered. They'd stopped coming by when Fort Macleod closed down.

"Yeah. It's easy. You just gotta stand at the edge of the road and wave your arms. Don't step out on the road, though. They drive fierce fast. They might run you down. You got that, Ian?"

He nodded. In spite of the sun his face was pale, his freckles standing out like star drifts, like the Milky Way. This time, when she gave his shoulder a comforting pat, he didn't flinch away from her. He's a fussy kid, she told herself. And he misses his Mom. And Charlie. She pushed her own feelings away again. I'll think about that later. Right now she had to concentrate on doing this right.

Bent double, low to the ground, she sidled down the slight slope toward the cliff edge. Halfway there she threw herself flat, took a breath, and looked around. Nobody. No movement. The sun was like a blow across her shoulders. The sweat ran into her eyes and she brushed her hand across her face.

There were the bedrolls, safe under the bush where she had left them, thank goodness. In another minute she'd have them safe. Then the possibility that Mike and the others—but especially Mike—might be hiding out of sight just below the cliff edge suddenly struck Megan. Again she wiped the sweat from her face. She forced herself to her feet. Only a few more yards.

Her heart was pounding, the noise in her ears like war drums. It got worse the closer she came to the cliff itself. She finally had to face the question she'd blocked from her mind up till this moment. Had Mike been going to push her over? As a sacrifice to Napi, maybe? Or was it just a crazy joke, getting a rise out of her? Her foot had been right on the crumbling edge when Ian's scream had pulled her back to reality. Perhaps Mike wouldn't have actually pushed her over, just allowed her to move forward in a sun-blinded trance until there was nothing beneath her feet anymore. Like the buffalo.

Here were the bedrolls. And the basket of chickens. Poor creatures, they'd be nearly dead of thirst by now, if they weren't already. First thing, she'd have to give them some water.

Water. She'd planned to fill their two canteens with the sweet water from the tap. Now it was too late. She'd missed her chance. Stupid. Stupid. Everything that could go wrong had gone wrong and they were still only a few miles from home. Maybe they should have stayed on the farm. Or walked to Lethbridge and asked for help, to be put in foster homes. No, never foster homes. She'd promised Mom to look after Ian, to stand by him.

She bit her lip, looking northeast, past the dark line of Mud Lake. She couldn't actually see the farm from here, though the empty irrigation canal, cutting the land like a ruled line, was clear enough. Over in the north the smoke she'd seen yesterday was thicker. And much farther east. Almost about to where the farm was. Where the farm would have been. By the time they got back they probably wouldn't have a roof over their heads anymore. The whole land was tinder dry and the house was wood, all except for the foundation.

She grabbed the bedrolls, the basket of chickens, and the canteens and, with no more thought of the possibility of Mike hiding, waiting to pounce on her, ran back to where Ian lay on the crest of the hill.

"Did you see anything move?"

"Nothing, Megan. Just ground squirrels."

"Okay then. Grab your bedroll and canteen and we'll head back to the slough. It's too hot to travel now. We'll wait it out till evening."

Ian turned and trotted obediently down the slope to the brush-edged slough.

"Hey, I said for you to carry your own canteen. I've only got two hands, you know."

"I've got it." He held it up. "Gee, it's heavy."

"Can't be. I never got the chance to . . ." Megan stopped, looked down at the two water bottles in her hand. Two full canteens. Three altogether. All of them full.

Mike's way of apologizing for Charlie, maybe? Or for what he'd tried to do at the buffalo jump? Maybe he'd been only a little crazy. Weren't they all, these days? But he'd sure made up for it. Three canteens filled with good spring water. Her dry lips cracked in a smile. "I guess we're okay, Ian. They're not after us anymore."

In the meager shade of the wolf willow, Megan opened the basket. One of the hens was already dead, the other two close to it, lying on their sides, their beaks opening and shutting spasmodically. She found a dried leaf scrolled into a funnel shape and painstakingly dripped water through it into the birds' open beaks. Only when they stopped gasping and scuttered to their feet did she allow herself one small swallow.

The water was cool, sweet, tangy. Incredible. She could have drunk it all. She imagined pouring it all over her head and shoulders. Firmly she screwed the cap on the bottle.

"Take it easy," she warned Ian. "If you finish that bottle today you won't get any more till we can refill it, and I don't know how long it'll be till we find good water. So make it last."

"I'm so thirsty, Megan. We'll come to a river soon, won't we? Now we're in the hills."

"I don't know. We can't count on it. Look at this slough. Dry as a bone, though there must have been a spring here once."

They lay in the diminishing shade, moving as little as possible, since every movement made them sweat the more. At last Megan felt a faint breeze coming up the rise from the west. "Let's go. We'll be cooler walking with it than lying here. Come on."

She set off confidently across the flat tabletop of the Porcupine Hills, keeping the sun and the dry creek to their left. After about an hour's walking they came to a wider stony-bottomed creek, also bone dry. Beyond it the ground fell away, and Megan could see a line of decaying fence posts, strung with wire.

"There'll be a road down there. Come on. It'll be easier walking now." Her heart rose. Maybe at last things were going right.

Tumbleweed had caught in the fence and sand drifted above the tumbleweed, almost to the top of the fence. They had to climb over wind-hardened dunes and trample down the two top wires in order to reach the road.

Megan was right. The westerly wind had scrubbed the road clear to its sand and rock base. Walking would be good, better than across country, with the continual fear of twisting an ankle in a hole or on a sagebrush root. The road curved northwesterly, but it was the only road there was and Megan felt certain it must be the right one.

Sure enough, after about an hour's walk, most of it uphill, the road turned definitely toward the west again.

"Can't we stop, Megan? It's so hot!"

"I know, Ian. Let's go just a bit farther. I want to find a place with a little shade and some wood, so we can have a fire and cook the chicken. An abandoned farm or a barn, maybe. We'll stop then, I promise."

The sun was low in the southwest now, blinding their eyes despite the turned-down brims of their hats. They almost missed the place because of the dazzle. It was just off the road to their right, the remains of a long-abandoned homestead, with sheds and outbuildings in various stages of decay. Megan dumped her bedroll on the northern side of the solidest-looking building—I wouldn't want it coming down on us during the night, she thought. The roof of the smallest shed had fallen in long ago, and the walls took only a tug to come apart into dry planks, perfect for a fire.

A stony area must have once been the lane to the homestead and here, mindful of the danger of grass-fires, Megan built her fire of tumbleweed starter, tinder-dry and brittle, with a tipi of broken planks above it. When she put a single match to it the tumbleweed caught in an explosion of flames.

"Keep feeding in the wood, Ian, till we get a good bed of red coals," she told him. Meanwhile, in the shade of the house, she plucked and gutted the dead hen, washed it out with the smallest amount of water possible, and cut off its head and feet.

By the time she was finished Ian had a solid pile of glowing embers, which he fed carefully, piece by piece, with broken planking. The sweat ran down his face, but he didn't complain.

"That's really great. I wish we could rig up something to hold it over the fire, kind of like a barbecue. That way we could roast it. It's a fatty bird, it'll roast good, and we'll save water."

"There's a junk heap over there." Ian left the fire and scampered off. He was back soon with half a dozen lengths of metal rod left over from some long-ago building project. They jammed two into the hard ground at each end of the fire, their tips crossed. X. The fifth Megan thrust through the gutted bird balanced in the notches of the crossed rods.

"We'll have to keep turning it, so it won't burn on one side and not cook on the other. You take a nap, Ian, and I'll watch it for a while."

Feeding the fire and watching that the bird didn't burn kept Megan from thinking. The sun dropped below the hills and the sky flushed brilliant red. Once the bird seemed to be cooked through, Megan woke Ian. She put the hen on a clean piece of plank and sawed off the breast meat, one big chunk for each of them. The skin was deliciously burned and the flesh juicy, though a bit tough. It wasn't a young bird, after all, Megan told herself. It had had a lifetime of egg-laying before it had come to this.

"I'll wrap up the legs for tomorrow," she said as she cut off a stringy wing for Ian to chew on. "We'll make an early start and eat as we walk along. Then when it gets too hot we'll rest. Okay?"

"I guess so."

They rubbed the grease off their fingers in the sand, had a small swallow of water, and then unrolled their blankets. The fire had died down and the stars, emerging one by one in the darkening sky, were comforting in their familiar patterns.

"Oh, look, Ian, a shooting star! And there's another. Make a wish, quick!"

"What are you wishing for, Megan? I—"

"Don't tell. It spoils it if you tell, remember?" In the darkness Megan's hand went to the crystal drop at her throat. I wish we can live beside the waterfall. Sweet water. Like in the calendar. In an instant's flash Megan could see the old kitchen, the stove, the jug on the table with the spoons and forks in it, the calendar on the wall, the shelves with their mismatched collection of dishes. Then it was gone.

She sighed. It was all behind them now. Gone. Probably burned up in that grass fire. Nothing left at all but ashes, like the ashes of this fire here. Mom and the baby deep in the sand of the irrigation canal. The fire'd leave them be, at least.

"Megan." Ian's voice came sleepily out of the darkness.

"Hmm?"

"Is there really a hole in the sky, like Mom used to tell us? 'Cause how come we can't see it? I mean, just look. There's stars everywhere, ain't there? No room for a hole."

"I dunno. Maybe it's kind of like a window that's got a little hole in it. When you look out you can see whatever's on the other side through the glass as well as through the hole, right? But the rain only comes in through the hole. And flies and wasps and suchlike. They can't come through the glass. I guess it's kinda like that."

She stared up at the sky, thinking about Mom . . .

"Megan?"

"Yeah?"

"Did Mom's soul go up thatta way? And the baby's? Through the hole in the sky?"

"I dunno, Ian. Maybe. Yeah, I guess so."

"But if Heaven's on the other side of that there hole, how come it's *bad* rays that come down and give people cancer and eye trouble?"

"I don't know, Ian. Hush up and go to sleep, do."

In the silence she heard him sigh and move restlessly from side to side. She propped herself up on her elbow. "What's the matter now?"

"Megan, d'you think Charlie'll go to Heaven?"

She bit her lip as unexpected tears pricked her eyes. She swallowed and made her voice strong, convincing. "You bet he will. Charlie was a good loyal dog and . . . and a friend. And in a way he gave his life for us, didn't he? To give us sustenance for the journey," she added as words from a long-ago prayer of Mom's leapt into her mind.

"Yeah." Ian's voice was sleepy, contented. He chuckled. "I hope there's lots of gophers in Heaven."

Megan lay awake and stared at the stars. Gee, it must

be great to be ten years old. No complications, no decisions to make. Growing up was tough. She found she was thinking about Mike Spotted Eagle. In her mind she could see his cleancut face with its high cheekbones and strong nose. And the strange eyes that gave nothing away of the person behind them. She'd never for a moment known what he was thinking. *Would* he have killed her? Let her walk off the cliff? Was the hand under her arm pushing or holding her back? She didn't know. She'd never know.

She shivered and her fingers moved to the comforting warmth of the crystal drop lying against her collar bone. With her hand on it she was able to fall asleep at last.

♦

"I'm so thirsty, Megan."

"We'll stop in a minute, Ian. At the top of that rise, okay?"

They had only been walking for about an hour, Megan reckoned. The sun was still low behind them so that their shadows walked ahead of them along the dirt road. But already Ian was tiring. Or maybe he was just grumbling, the way he did with her.

As they came to the top of the slight rise, they could see the land fall away before them. There, ahead of them, was the long line of the Rockies, like jagged saw teeth against the cloudless sky. Megan strained her eyes for snow, for glaciers. Mom had said there were places where the snow never melted, even in summer. Was that a glint on that peak over there?

"Look. You can see where we're heading, Ian. See that white up there? Snow. In the middle of summer, imagine. Think of the snow they must get in wintertime, enough to make the grass come up green in the spring, I bet."

Ian wasn't interested in the scenery. "I'm thirsty," he said again. There was a real whine in his voice, and Megan could feel irritation rise in her, prickling like the heat.

"Well, have a sip of water, silly billy. Only go carefully. I don't know when we'll be able to refill the canteens."

"There's no more left."

"What!" Megan snatched his canteen, shook it, and held it disbelievingly upside down. "Oh, *honestly*, Ian!"

"I was thirsty. That chicken leg just made me thirstier."

Reluctantly Megan handed him the extra canteen, the one that Mike had left for them. "Just a sip, mind. I'm saving this one for emergencies. We haven't passed a single creek that's had water in it. Hey, I said just a swallow. Give it back." She reached out.

"Gee, you're mean. Mean and bossy. Here, take your stupid canteen." He pushed it into her hands so clumsily that precious water splashed from it and fell to the sandy road.

"Oh, Ian, how can you be so dumb?" Almost in tears, Megan screwed the top on the canteen and slung it over her shoulder. She licked a few precious drops that had fallen on her hand and rubbed the damp hand over her forehead. For a small second the westerly wind cooled her face. Then the water evaporated and the wind was as hot and dry as ever. She turned on him.

"You're hopeless! You're just a selfish baby and I don't know why I bother!"

She strode down the road, Ian half a dozen paces behind her, dragging his feet in the dust. The trail led downhill now and she could see, like the relief map in Napi's world, the road meander ahead of them. It seemed to turn northwest again, to become lost in a fold of low foothills, which was worrying. But it was all right. Soon she could see, no more than half a mile ahead of them, a road running due south, a more important-looking road, laid straight out across the land as if with a ruler.

"That's our way, Ian." She pointed and turned. He'd fallen even farther behind and was dragging his feet. His lower lip stuck out and he dragged his feet through the dust with every step. How did Mom deal with him? Did he have sulks back then? When Mom was alive. Or was it *her*? What was she doing wrong?

"Look." She tried to talk cheerfully as he came level with her. "See, that's the road we're going to take."

"How d'you know? You haven't got a map or nothing."

"The land's like a map, isn't it? You can see over there, the gap in the Rockies. It's clear as clear. That's Crowsnest Pass. Lundbreck's on the way to it."

"I don't want to go. I want to go home. You don't know where we're going, what's going to be there, do you? You're just making it up. Dreaming. That's all."

Megan tried to keep her temper. "We can't go home, Ian. There's nothing there. The well was running dry, you know that. And remember the smoke we saw day before yesterday, north of the Porcupine Hills? Well, when I went to pick up our bedrolls I saw it again. Grass fire all right. Real close to the farm. By now it'll all be burned up, and so'd we be, if we'd stayed on."

She had a sudden vision, as she spoke, of the lace curtains in the kitchen window slowly turning black, their pattern still clear, and then crumbling into black dust. She imagined the calendar on the wall, its shiny paper shriveling, curling up toward the forever-falling water.

"There *is* no home anymore, Ian," she said finally. "There's only going on. We don't have any choice. And west makes more sense than east. West is where there's water."

His lip trembled. Had she been too hard on him? When he again asked for water she handed him the spare canteen without argument. He sloshed water into his mouth, screwed on the cap, and slung the canteen over his shoulder. Then he walked defiantly down the road.

"Okay," she yelled after him. "Just you remember, when that's gone there ain't no more."

She shook her own canteen. Less than half full. She took a small mouthful, holding it in her mouth, letting it wet her dry lips, before she let it trickle down her throat. She squatted down, opened the hens' basket, and dribbled water into their upturned beaks. She had let them loose the previous night to peck around the abandoned farm and roost on one of the beams, and they were more healthy and cheerful-looking today.

Guess I'll hang on to them. We'll have a stew of that dried gopher meat tonight, she thought. So I'd better not drink anymore. I'll need the water for the stew. *My* water. *My* ration. She looked at Ian, strutting down the road with the spare canteen over his shoulder. She felt angry and ill-done-by. And hot.

With an exasperated sigh she slung bedroll and canteen over her shoulder and picked up the hens' basket. I wish I could have a bath. Wash my hair and my clothes. My teeth are gritty and I stink of sweat. Mom'd be ashamed of me.

She trudged down the road until she caught up with Ian, waiting at the fork in the road. "This way," she said confidently and turned south. This was a more important road, wide enough for cars to pass each other. The westerly wind had blown tumbleweed against the barbed-wire fence, and sand had drifted up nearly to the top strand of wire, but the roadway itself was almost clear. Only in patches, where the fence had broken down, were there drifts of sand across the road. There were no car tracks and no footprints except their own.

The road ran straight south, mounting small sandy hills and dipping down into places were there had once been creeks. There were white patches leaching out of the sand here and there, and a few tufts of coarse alkaline grass. So even if there had been water, it would not have been drinkable.

What'll we do tomorrow? The thought pounded through Megan's head as she walked. Over and over: When the water's gone, what'll we do?

At the top of a slight rise she stopped to take off her cotton hat and let the wind cool her forehead and sweat-dampened hair. With so little to drink, in this parching heat, she wondered why her body kept making sweat.

She glanced over to the right. There was a wide low valley and, on its farther side, a meandering line of green scrub. *Green.* A creek with good water.

Her first inclination was to scramble over the fence and run downhill into the valley, but common sense held her back. There'll be a road. There's bound to be a farmhouse down there. And that means a road. We can ask for shelter and the use of their water in exchange for one of the hens. They'll let us bathe in the creek. Wash our clothes. Fill our canteens to the brim.

"Come on, Ian." She straightened her shoulders. "Over there. *Water.*"

It took them about an hour to get to the turnoff. There was a gate with a sign on it and beyond the gate a single-lane dirt road.

"What's that board say?"

"Tres-passers will be . . . something. There's long words I don't know. Doesn't matter. Come on."

They climbed the fence and set off along the track. The sun was high, beating down relentlessly on their heads. Their shadows no longer danced encouragingly ahead. There was no place to rest on the way. No gully. No dry creekbed. No tree.

"But it can't be far now, Ian. That was green brush we saw back there."

The road turned abruptly southward and downhill and, suddenly, there to their left, was the creek, running clean over pebbles, rippling in curds of white foam around bigger stones. The farm wasn't in sight. Probably up the hill and around the next bend.

"Come on. We'll get cleaned up and fill our water bottles. Then we'll go find the farmhouse. Let's go!"

Megan stomped down the lower strands of barbed wire that edged the roadway so that Ian could crawl through. Then she handed over the hens' basket and tossed over her bedroll before following him. This place was definitely inhabited. The fence posts were in good trim and the barbed wire new and unrusty.

Down the slope toward the creek the sage grew lavishly, the wind flattening it so that it shimmered in silver-gray waves, like a lake of clear water. The tangy scent tickled her nostrils and made her head swim.

And there was the creek. Almost ten yards wide. Not very deep. Even in the middle the water still riffled over the stony bottom. It was as clear as . . . as her crystal drop. Megan dropped her bedroll and the basket and simply stared, until she became aware of Ian tearing off his shoes and socks.

"Hey, wait a minute. Let me fill the canteens first, before you start stirring it up and getting our drinking water all muddy."

She stripped off her own shoes and socks and waded ankle-deep into the water, holding the bottles carefully so that only the freshly flowing water filled them. Only after she'd waded back to shore did she let Ian strip off his clothes and fling himself into the water.

"Hey, Megan, look at me." He lay on his stomach, facing upstream, damming the flow so that the water bubbled up over his shoulders and down his back.

"We can't stay long," Megan warned him. "We mustn't let ourselves get sunburned."

"That darned hole," Ian grumbled and rolled on his back, kicking spray up into the hot air.

Megan stripped off her own clothes and crouched in the water, gasping as it hit her hot body. She unplaited her wiry braids and washed the dust and sweat out of her hair. I just wish I'd thought to bring soap, she thought. But Mom's lye soap sat in a tin on the kitchen sink, too soft to pack anyway.

After she'd washed her hair she rinsed out their shirts, socks, and underpants and laid them on top of the sagebrush. In a couple of hours they'd be bone dry.

"I'm not going to wash your jeans or my skirt, though. They'd just take too long to dry, even in this heat."

Among the brush growing along the creekside they found saskatoons ripe enough to eat and filled themselves with the berries. Then, in the shade of the brush, they dozed through the heat of the afternoon.

"Let's stay here all night, Meg," Ian begged when they woke up in the twilight. "Let's not go on yet."

"Well, maybe just tonight. There's lots of driftwood for a fire. And a stony beach so it'll be safe. I was planning gopher stew. I'll put in fresh berries and it'll be real good."

After the stew was bubbling on the fire Megan looked up the darkening road. "I really should go up to the farmhouse I saw and tell them who we are, so they won't be nervous about strangers camping on their land."

"It's getting dark. We'll be going right past their place in the morning," Ian suggested.

"Yeah. Morning'll be time enough." Megan lay on her blanket, spread on the soft young sage close to the creek, and sighed happily. There had been moments in the last days when her decision to go west instead of east had seemed totally stupid. The moment she'd realized the craziness of Mike; when she'd stood at the edge of the buffalo jump; the death of Charlie; when they'd nearly run out of water.

But it had turned out all right. Everything was great. They'd found water at last and Ian hadn't whined about anything for hours.

It was almost dark now. She stirred the stew. Good enough. She stirred up the embers and put on another piece of driftwood before putting the hot pot down between them. "Just don't burn your mouth."

The meat was tender, sparked with the acid freshness

of the berries. Maybe not quite as good as barbecued hen, but not bad at all. So long as there's water we're all right, she thought. We can catch ground squirrels with string traps and we can roast grasshoppers, I guess. They do in Africa. I read it in a book. And for now, well, we've come better'n a third of the way. The canteens are full, we've two hens left and it's going to be all right.

She got up to rinse off the pot and their spoons and then rolled herself up in her blanket. Above her the stars twinkled reassuringly.

"Good night, Ian. Sleep well."

"Good night, Megan. Meg . . ."

"Yeah?"

"That stew was okay."

Megan smiled in the darkness. That was probably as close as she'd get to an apology from a kid brother. She turned on her side, the smell of sage drifting over her, and slept.

FIVE

Megan was dreaming about Charlie, somehow miraculously alive again. He'd followed them from the Porcupine Hills and now he'd caught up with them. He was on the bank above her head, barking a noisy welcome.

She opened her eyes sleepily to a dazzle of sun shining through the brush. The barking was still going on, but it wasn't Charlie's hysterical "I love you and isn't the gopher-hunting great today." This was a series of short measured barks with a low gargling snarl between each. It was not friendly.

Cautiously she rolled on to her front and looked up. On the bank just above her stood a smooth-haired dog with an ugly blunt muzzle, its feet braced against a restraining leash. With each bark the dog strained forward. With each snarl it curled back its lip to show long white sharp canines.

Megan's eyes took in the polished riding boots beside the dog and traveled slowly up to breeches, a belted jacket of what looked like some kind of uniform. At the top a face, smoothly shaven, unlined, unsmiling, the eyes shaded by a visored cap.

"Ian," she whispered. "*Ian!*" She kicked desperately at the sleeping bundle beside her, hoping that no sudden movement would set off either dog or owner. "Ian, wake *up*." He grunted sleepily. "Get up *slowly*. Get your gear together *now*. We've got company."

Cautiously she got to her knees. The dog's barking increased and it pulled eagerly on the leash. Megan felt her mouth go dry. She got to her feet, stepping back hastily so that there was more space between them.

"Good morning, sir. We were just resting on our way west. We've done no damage."

"You used our water, didn't you?"

"Y-yes, of course. We'd have died without it. But we're downstream from your farm, doing no harm. Just washing and filling our canteens."

"Stop acting the innocents. You're on private property. You saw the signs. Can't you read?"

Megan flushed. "Sure I can read. But not real long words. I didn't know what the signs meant. I'm sorry if—"

"Gee, why's your dog mad at us? If we still had Charlie I bet he'd show you!"

"Hush up, Ian. Get your bedroll together. *Now.* Make sure you fasten it properly. Remember the difference between a slip knot and a bowline? So do it." Megan kept her voice low and her eyes still on man and dog. If only Ian'd pay attention to what she said without getting into an argument. "We're on our way right now, sir."

Quickly she tossed her dry shirt and socks, the cooking pot and knife and spoons into her blanket. She rolled it up, tied it, and got slowly to her feet again.

"We were coming up to your place to say we'd stayed overnight. We'd have come last evening, but we were that tired."

"If you'd have come up to our place you'd have been shot," the man said shortly. "We're not keen on strangers coming by."

"No, sir. Sorry, sir." She spoke automatically, while her brain slowly took in his words. Shot? Surely he was joking? But his face was stern, unmoving. Like it was carved out of sandstone. The dog had stopped barking, but was watching them intently, its lips drawn back to show teeth and gums, a low noise in its throat like a pot just coming to the boil.

"Ready, Ian? Got your canteen? Come on, then." She took a step forward to the bank. The dog growled and she saw the short hair on its shoulders bristle. "If you'll just let us by, sir, we'll be on our way."

"The road's private. The land is ours. I thought I made that quite clear."

"Yes, but . . . it's a public road. It goes west, the way we've got to go."

"The law's different now. Our signs are up, saying this is our place. No one goes by. *No* one. Clear?"

"But what d'you want us to do then?" Megan was almost in tears, partly of rage, partly of frustration.

"You want to go west, go west, then. That way." He gestured across the creek. Then he bent to loosen the dog's chain. "*Now.*"

Megan screamed, "Ian, quick." She grabbed her bedroll and the other two canteens and pulled Ian by the hand, splashing across the creek and scrambling up the farther bank.

"Megan, I forgot my hat."

"Oh, Ian!" Megan turned reluctantly back. At once the man released the dog, which bounded through the water toward them, throwing up a wall of spray through which she glimpsed an open mouth and shining canines.

"Come on, Ian, run! Fast as you can!"

Together they pounded across the dry ground, expecting to feel the savage bite of teeth, the tearing of cloth and flesh. Then Megan, her arms full of bedroll and canteens, tripped over an unseen sage root and went sprawling. "Go on," she gasped, trying to get back her wind, but Ian turned and stood above her, swinging his canteen in front of him like a weapon.

"It's okay, Meg. I won't let him getcha."

As she staggered to her feet, gasping, she heard the throaty growl of the dog almost in her ear. She turned in time to see it leap, mouth snarling. Then Ian's swinging canteen crashed into the side of its head. Her scream blended with the sound of a shrill whistle. The dog shook its head, turned, and loped off.

"You okay, Meg?" Ian's voice wobbled uncertainly.

She pulled herself to her feet. The palms of her hands were skinned and she licked them clean.

"Yeah. I'm fine. Let's get out of here before he changes his mind."

She slung her bedroll over one shoulder, the two canteens over the other, and limped grimly on, Ian at her side. The sun beat down. They had slept late and now it wasn't far off noon.

"You'd better wear my hat, Ian."

"Then what'll you do?"

"You're fairer than I am. Take it."

They trudged over the rough ground in silence for a while. "It's my fault," Megan said at last. "I should have thought. Water's that precious I guess people guard it like . . . like money in the bank."

"That man was crazy, wasn't he, Meg?"

She nodded. "I guess so. A little bit anyway."

"D'you suppose everyone we meet's gonna be like that?"

"Maybe. We'll just have to be extra careful. Like we're in enemy territory." He looked frightened. "Kind of like a game," she added.

He still seemed unhappy.

"Well, what's the problem?"

"When we get to that place we're going to . . . suppose they're like that there too?"

Megan shook her head. The question was unanswerable. Also she found that she was needing all her breath for walking. They had left the sagebrush behind and were climbing steadily up sandy stony ground, bare except for clumps of speargrass, the barbed seeds of which broke off and stuck to their socks, working through the fabric to prick their ankles viciously.

"Well, aren't you going to tell me?" His voice went up. "Why're we going if'n folks are going to be like that where we're going? Megan?"

"Ian, I just don't know. But . . ."

"But what?"

"We're doing the best we can, aren't we? We gotta trust it'll work out. Come on, don't look so down. You were *great* back there. I guess you just about saved my life."

A smile wavered across his face and vanished.

"Come on, Ian. The high bit's over there. And after that it'll be downhill."

They stopped for breath at the top, seeing the road shimmer ahead of them, ruler-straight toward the mountains. Then they both looked back. Toward the green line that marked the beautiful creek where they had spent the night. They couldn't see the farmhouse, but a few low structures, with domed roofs like silos, were just visible among the trees.

"What d'you suppose those are, Megan?"

"I remember Dad talking about people building houses underground, filling them with dried food and stuff, so they could hole up for years. He said they were called—what was it?—yeah, survivalists. I bet that's what these guys are."

"What's *survivalist* mean?"

"I guess people who want to survive."

"I thought everyone did that."

"I guess maybe they'll kill to survive. Maybe that's the difference."

They came to the road at last. Here the fence posts were rotted, the barbed wire rusted and sagging, very different from the road to the survivalists' place. They tromped down the wire and climbed over easily.

"What'll we do if we meet someone else? Someone like *him*?" Ian's voice wobbled.

"Hey, you're not scared, are you? C'mon! After the way you stood up for me when I tripped and we thought the dog was gonna get us? Anyway, think about it. We haven't met a single soul on the roads since we left home. I think the roads are safe. But we'll be real careful when we get close to any buildings, especially if there's good water nearby. That's where there'll be trouble."

They walked silently on, through the unending clatter of grasshopper and cricket. The land shimmered in the heat and Megan could feel the sun drawing the newfound moisture out of her skin, tightening it against her flesh. Her head, now she no longer had a hat, was beginning to pound. When they stopped for a careful sip of water, she took her spare shirt from her bedroll bundle and draped it over her head and shoulders.

As she slung the bedroll over one shoulder and the canteens over the other, she suddenly stopped and looked down at her hands. "This is crazy. Something's missing. The hens! Oh, Ian, I forgot the basket of hens!"

"Never mind, Meg. You couldn't have gone back for them. That there dog woulda chewed you up."

"We've got nothing but a bit of gopher meat left. Not much of that and it's beginning to smell a bit funny. Oh, I wish we'd eaten one of those hens last night! Now those horrid survivalists will have them both!"

Ian chuckled suddenly. "Now you can't go on being mad at me for forgetting my hat, can you?"

"I wasn't mad at you, silly. And you were real brave, standing by me when I tripped. What would you have done if the dog *had* come after us?"

He didn't answer.

She scowled, anxiety at his innocence blotting out her concern over the chickens. "Well, you just listen to me, Ian Dougal. If anything like that happens to me again you've got to *run*. Run like heck and don't wait up for me."

"But—"

"Listen. I didn't tell you this before, but when Mom was dying I promised her I'd look out for you. Now she's gone it's like I'm your mom and you've got to mind me. Okay? So I'm telling you, if anything goes wrong, you just run."

"Okay, bossy. You don't have to go on. I heard you." He stomped off, his worn canvas shoes scuffing up the dirt.

Megan sighed. Darn. She tried, but somehow she

never seemed to be able to handle him right, the way Mom would have done. But she had to tell him, and she had to make it stick. That dog could have chewed Ian into little pieces if the man hadn't blown his whistle in time.

She looked after him, stomping ahead of her down the road, with feelings that mixed exasperation and loving. Then she frowned. Now that he was ahead of her, she could see that something was wrong with his arm. "Ian, wait up."

He walked on as if he hadn't heard.

"Ian!" She broke into a run and caught up with him. "Ian, did you catch your arm on the barbed wire?"

" 'S nothing." He tried to twist away, but she grabbed his forearm.

"It's only a scratch, but was it on the wire? Rusty wire's dangerous, Mom said."

"Nope. It was that darn dog if you want to know."

"Why didn't you tell me? I should clean it."

"Thought you'd get mad at me again." Tears trickled down his cheeks, making runnels in the dust.

"Oh, Ian love, why'd I do that? You saved my life, didn't you? Now you sit right down on your bundle till I fix this up."

She wetted the hem of her spare shirt from the canteen and washed the scratch thoroughly.

"I think it's okay. Does it hurt a lot?"

"Some."

"Oh, Ian, I dunno. I guess I just don't understand you. Sometimes you're a just a great baby, and sometimes you're as brave as . . . as a lion." She hugged him.

He grinned faintly, but his face looked pinched and his eyes had that white flash of fear she'd seen in them before.

"What's the matter? You still don't trust me to get you safe to Uncle Greg's?"

" 'Tain't that."

"Then what is it, for pete's sake?"

He suddenly burst into tears, sobs shaking his whole body. She held him tight, feeling again that dangerous softness, the softness that might get in the way of her hard will to reach Lundbreck.

"What is it then?"

"Am I going to go mad, Megan?"

"What?"

"Dog bites make you go mad, don't they? You foam at the mouth and run around in circles and they have to shoot you. Dad told me."

She couldn't help laughing at that, and he pulled himself out of her arms, his face stiff and offended.

"I'm sorry. I didn't mean— It's all right, Ian, honest. You only get sick like that if the dog that bit you's got it. That dog that scratched you wasn't sick mad. He was mad mad. You'll be okay."

"Honest?"

"Honest, cross my heart. Look, Ian. Down there. There's an old farmhouse just about buried in sand. When we get there we'll have a rest and a bit of a meal, okay?"

They climbed the rotting fence and hunkered down in the shady northeast corner of an old shed. Megan unwrapped the last of their food. A couple of strips of dried meat and a half a round of flat-bread. As she broke the bread in two, she felt a sudden pang of longing for their own kitchen, the stove, for the water, however alkaline, that still dribbled from their own pump. I wish I were home, she thought. I wish I hadn't brought us here into this desert.

Then she made herself hard again and held out a strip of meat and half the bread to Ian. "Here's dinner," she said cheerfully.

"I can't eat this. It ain't cooked."

"Sure it is. Sun-dried. It's fine. You just tear off a little bit and chew it."

"It's too dry. I want a drink."

"You mean you've finished yours again?"

She swallowed her impatience and handed him the extra canteen. "Take it slow. Just little sips."

She watched his throat move. He looked at her over the edge of the canteen, just daring her to grab it back. I won't play that game again, she told herself, and turned away, staring back up the road down which they'd come.

"Getting more water's going to be difficult," she said after she'd got her temper under control. "Well, you know what happened last time. I think what we're going to have to do is to go on walking as long as we possibly can. If we find good water and there aren't any houses nearby, that's great. We're probably safe enough. But if we find water and there's folks living nearby, we're going to have to hide out till it's really dark. The middle of the night. Then I'll sneak over and fill our canteens and we'll go by their place in the dark till we're safely out of reach. Then we'll sleep. Okay?"

Ian grunted. I guess he's still mad at me for laughing at him, Megan thought. The grasshoppers whirred in the dusk. What do they find to eat? she wondered. There's not a speck of green. The hot dry silence bore down on her.

"I'll help you fill the canteens." Ian broke the silence at last.

"Thanks, Ian. But I think I'd better do it myself."

"I'm not a baby, Megan Dougal. You keep treating me like I'm a baby. I'm *ten years old!*"

"I know, silly. I didn't mean— It's just that it'll be a lot quieter for one person sneaking up. And you've got that sore arm. You . . ." She racked her brain for the right words. "You can keep watch. Let me know that everything's quiet. That's every bit as important, you know. Okay?"

"I guess so," he said grudgingly.

"All right. We've had our rest and something to eat. We'd better go on if you're okay."

At the end of the next bend the land opened up on their right, falling away to disclose a wide shallow valley, at the center of which they could clearly see a dark line of vegetation.

"See over there? Water! I bet there's a road going that way."

Sure enough, a little farther on they could see the faint mark of a trail branching westward. "We'll go that way. It's bound to cross the creek."

"I think I see a building. Over there." Ian pointed.

"Can you tell if it's lived in? Or is it just another old barn?"

"Can't see from here."

"I don't think we should risk the road. There's quite a bit of light left. Anyone looking this way . . . let's get off the road, into the brush. We'll rest till it's really dark."

They crouched among the clumps of perfumed sage, waiting for the slow summer evening to turn to night. Megan felt the tiredness in her bones and muscles, felt her eyes slowly shut. She forced them open again. It would be awful to fall asleep and not waken till morning, to have to look for water in broad daylight, not knowing when men with vicious dogs might jump out at them.

The sky slowly darkened. The evening star gleamed brightly over the distant mountains. A long way off a lone coyote howled sadly. Or was it a dog? Megan shivered and waited and watched.

Suddenly a square of light blinked into view and as quickly vanished as a window was shuttered. She sat up, her arms encircling her knees, and watched and waited. The evening star set in the west and the moon rose behind them. Almost full. The moon was a pity, but it couldn't be helped.

At last, when she was sure that whoever lived in that house must be asleep, she shook Ian awake, her hand over his mouth in case he should shout out.

"We'll creep along the left side of the road, opposite to the house," she explained when he was properly awake. "In case we have to run for it. When I stay to fill up the canteens at the creek, you go on with the bedrolls. Don't stop for anything till you're out of sight of the house, up the road over there, on the far side. That's really important, Ian. If you hear any kind of fuss, you just run. Don't come back. I'll catch up with you."

The darkness seemed to have knocked the spunk and fight out of Ian. He didn't argue, just nodded, his face pale in the moonlight, his eyes dark and shadowed.

"Right," said Megan firmly, a great deal more confidently than she felt. "Off we go, then."

They moved as quietly as they could along the edge of the road, Megan in the lead, bent over so as to make as unnoticeable a silhouette in the moonlight as possible, supposing someone should look out of one of the windows over there.

After a time they didn't have to crouch down, because a high embankment carried the road over the creek, and in its shadow they were completely hidden. Megan straightened her aching back thankfully.

She took Ian's canteen and handed him her bedroll. "Just remember what I told you. Stay on this side of the road till you're way past the house and out of sight. And for pete's sake, keep quiet!" she hissed as his feet suddenly clattered on stones at the bottom of the creek.

"Meg, it's dry."

"It can't be, silly billy. Look how green everything is. Off you go now."

She waited until he was safely up the slope before she knelt down to fill the canteens. Her knees felt dry boulders. She put the flat of her hand on the creek bottom. Ian had been right! There was only a trickle among the stones. Enough to moisten her lips, to wet the hem of her skirt. Not nearly enough to fill the canteens.

Panic swept over Megan. Without water they

couldn't survive long, not in this heat. They could eat grasshoppers. Catch ground squirrels. But without water they'd die.

She slumped down on the creek bottom, her forehead against the stones. So much for her promise to Mom. She'd dragged Ian away from whatever safety there might have been in Lethbridge to perish in the hills looking for a crazy dream.

The crystal drop, hung on its nylon thread around her neck, swung forward, sparkling in the moonlight, like a great drop of water. Her lucky crystal. Her fingers wrapped around it and, as she moved, her eye was caught by something odd.

The road had been built straight across the creekbed to the house, over an earth embankment, so that the road was perhaps ten or twelve feet above the creek at this spot. A huge culvert had been imbedded in this embankment to take the flow of water downstream. She could see moon glints on the small puddles close by. Looking through the culvert, she ought to be able to see the moon glinting on the water on the other side. But she didn't. All she could see when she peered through the culvert was blackness.

She sat back on her heels and thought about it. She could see Ian's shadowy figure over on the other side of the creek, climbing the far bank. She waited until he was safely out of sight. Then she crept up to the entrance to the culvert and peered in. There could be a huge animal in there, blocking out the light. She swallowed and went closer, her heart pounding. But it was all right. Once she was close she could see, in the clear moonlight, that some kind of structure lay between her and the expected view of moonlight on water.

She slipped the canteens from her shoulder and began to wriggle through the culvert, pushing them ahead of her. The culvert was at least thirty feet long, and it was very dark. Its bottom was slimy wet against her bare knees. At least the slime made crawling through easier, she thought, suppressing a shudder.

Her breath echoed harshly. It was like the sound of some wild animal. Her heart thudded against her ribs, pressed painfully against the bottom of the culvert.

She took a steadying breath and shuffled forward, pushing the canteens ahead of her. Now it was no longer totally dark. Ahead was something like a wall, filling up the lower two-thirds of the circular frame of the culvert. In the upper third were stars, winking comfortingly at her. Unthinkingly she raised her head and hit it on the metal edge.

"Ow!" Megan wriggled the rest of her body through, stood up, and rubbed her head. Now it all made sense. The wall that had hidden her view of the creek upstream was a dam, a couple of yards high, built of stones and dirt, stretching the full width of the creekbed. A little water trickled slowly over the spillway, threads of silver slowly meandering downstream. And behind the dam must be a lake. A whole wonderful lakeful of precious water.

She looked over to her left. From her position at the very bottom of the creek, she could no longer see the house or outbuildings. Neither, for that matter, could anyone see her. Which was fine, except that to reach the water she would have to climb one or other bank.

She thought about possible dogs and shivered. The more she thought about them the more impossible it became to move at all. But then she remembered Ian, waiting for her somewhere along the road behind the house. Wondering what was happening. She told herself that the longer she waited the higher the moon would climb. Soon it would be like a great white yard light rubbing out all the night shadows, the safe hiding places. Soon there would be nowhere left to hide. She'd better move now.

Slowly she crawled up the west bank, keeping as low as possible. She chose the west bank because, though it brought her dangerously close to the house and its unknown inhabitants, it also brought her closer to her escape route along the road. If they did discover her and she was on the eastern bank, they could block the road and cut her off from Ian.

So she gritted her teeth and climbed the west bank, to be rewarded by the gleam of smooth water behind the brimming dam, the moon reflected in a perfect silver circle in its midst. Flat on her stomach, she unscrewed the first canteen and sank it in the water, its narrow opening half below the surface. She felt it filling, growing heavier in her hand. The reflection of the moon shivered and broke apart into a hundred dancing crystal drops. She screwed the top back on and filled the second canteen.

She had just pushed the last canteen below the surface of the water when the light went on. It was brilliantly white, far outshining the moon, and it came from somewhere behind her.

Without thinking she looked toward it, her night-accustomed eyes instantly blinded. She turned away quickly, her hand to her eyes, and the third canteen slipped out of her grasp. She grabbed at it, her fingers just touching the edge of the strap as it sank beneath the water.

She snatched up the two remaining canteens and scrambled up the steep embankment to the road. The fence posts at the top were new, the barbed wire springy and taut. She dove between the second and third strands, felt the wire catch and hold her hair, the back of her shirt.

She lunged desperately through it, the whole weight of her body against the restraining wires, her mind full of one thought only. Guard dogs. It seemed, when she remembered it, that from the instant of the light being switched on to the sound of tearing cloth was a single frozen moment of white light and silence.

Then there was a kind of interior click and time began to run normally again. She could hear men's voices shouting. She was free of the fence. She was running along the road westward, the canteens, grasped in her left hand by their straps, banging against her side.

Now she was under the tall post from which hung the cluster of yard lights. Now she was past the first building.

"Stop! Stop thief!"

Human voices. No dogs. Yet. She pounded along the trail, her wet skirt clinging, wrapping itself around her thighs, her feet in their thin canvas shoes slapping wetly against the surface of the road. She clenched her hand around the straps of the canteens. I'll never let go of them. Never. And she mourned for the canteen that had slipped out of her hand and sunk to the bottom of the pool.

Her foot turned sideways on a hidden stone and she

slipped, staggered, and regained her balance just as a sound like an angry bee whipped past her cheek. A bee? In the middle of the night? Hundreds of miles from any flowers?

That was a *bullet*, she realized, in a slow thought that seemed to have nothing to do with her body, which had recovered its balance and was running on. She felt only extreme astonishment. *They are shooting at me.*

Now she was past the last of the outbuildings. Her moon shadow danced like a crazy puppet along the trail ahead of her. Another bullet whined by. The stitch in her side was tearing her in two. She could no longer feel her feet against the stony ground. She felt as if she were running in a dream. Slow, slower. Like running through a great flat dish of molasses.

In her imagination, enemy feet were just behind her, catching up with great, impossibly long strides. Now a hand would be reaching out to catch her by the shoulder, spin her around, tear the canteens of precious water from her grasp. "No!" she gasped through her clenched teeth. "No!"

The ground was rising more slowly ahead of her. The moonlight lit up the crest of the hill over to her right. Once over the top, she'd be out of sight. Surely they wouldn't pursue her that far just for the sake of two canteensful of stolen water.

She felt a blow to her right arm and stumbled, looking over her shoulder. Surprisingly there was no one behind her. Nobody was reaching out to grab her. The road behind was empty and, as she spun around, the yard light went out. Down by the creek everything was dark and quiet.

She turned again. The soft moon lit up the road. It was only a few hundred yards to the top of the rise, Megan guessed. If he'd done as she'd said, Ian should be waiting for her with the bedrolls. They could walk for maybe another hour, just to be sure. It was as clear as daylight on the road.

She stumbled. Watch it! She was tired, that was all. In an hour they'd stop and sleep, maybe sleep right through the heat of the next day, and walk on again in the cool of evening under the pleasant moonlight.

How heavy the canteens were! She tried to sling them over her left shoulder, but the hand that held the straps tightly twisted around it wouldn't let go. She stumbled on, weaving drunkenly from left to right, tripping over sand drifts and the occasional clump of speargrass. She could hear the breath gasping in and out of her dry mouth. She licked her lips. It'd be good to stop, just long enough to take a drink. No, she told herself. Not till I catch up to Ian. And we'll have to be so careful. Only two canteens now.

When she reached the top of the rise, her feet followed each other automatically along the downslope. It's lucky it's downhill, she thought. So tired. Almost at the end of . . . but I can't stop now. They're after me again. I can hear their voices, calling me to stop. I won't. *I won't.*

She tried to run, but her legs felt as if they were in rubber boots filled with water. Picking up each one and pushing it forward took so much energy . . . more than she had . . .

"Megan! Megan, stop!"

Wasn't that Ian's voice? Or were they tricking her? Trying to catch her by pretending to be her brother. She ran on.

"Megan!" He was crying. It *was* Ian.

She stopped and turned. There were no pursuers. Only one small figure, laden down with bedrolls, running down the moonlit road after her.

"Why didn't you wait? Didn't you hear me? What's the matter?"

She shook her head dumbly and stood, her shoulders heaving, trying to catch her breath, her arms hanging limply at her side, the canteen straps wound so tightly around her left hand that the flesh had swollen around them.

"Megan, what's that?"

The horror in Ian's voice penetrated the cocoon of tiredness that wrapped her around. She looked down, following the direction of Ian's pointing finger. She saw her right hand, streaked dark, saw black spots falling from the fingers to the moonlit road. Like rain falling. Bloody rain.

"Ian." She wanted to tell him what he must do, but her tongue was so swollen, her mouth so dry. She took a step toward him and felt the road move, rise up, and sweep her away into blackness.

SIX

Ian felt his feet kick dry pebbles on the creekbed. They clattered noisily in the still air.

"For pete's sake, keep quiet," Megan hissed at him.

"Meg, it's dry."

"It can't be, silly billy. Look how green everything is. Off you go now."

He felt his way across the creek bottom, the weight of their bundles cutting into his shoulders. It was hard walking quietly across the loose stones. It *is* dry, stupid, he wanted to shout. Bossy Megan.

Once on the other side, he was able to move more

quietly through sage and grass up the slope to the left of the track. He could see the farm dwellings as faint shadows now, over to his right. A two-story farmhouse, with a barn, an open implement shed, and a couple of small buildings clustered behind it. A metal storage silo gleamed silvery in the light of the rising moon.

Safe in the shelter of a patch of brush, he looked to see how Megan was managing to fill the canteens at a creek with no more than a trickle of water going through it. It would serve her right, wouldn't it, if there wasn't any water, he thought spitefully. But then there would be nothing more to drink. And without water they'd die, that was for sure. He sighed. Everything was muddled in his mind nowadays. Like knowing they had to go easy on water, but being darned if Megan was going to ration it for him. Like wanting to get safely to Uncle Greg's, but sick and tired of Megan telling him how they were going to do it. As if he were a little kid.

The moon shone round and white on a pond that was deep enough to drown in. He could see how the creek ran into it from the left, and he could see how the dam cut off the flow on the right, just above the culvert that went under the road. Megan seemed to have vanished. He strained his eyes into the darkness, staring into the moon shadows by the culvert. The hard stone inside him grew heavier, the weight that had been there almost every moment since Megan had sent him off gopher-hunting with Charlie and he'd come home to find that Mom and the new baby were dead. If Megan was gone, what was he to do? It was all very well for her to tell him to go south till he came to the highway and then get a car to stop. But what then? What would he do? Who would he be? He wasn't even sure who he was right now. He wrapped his arms across his chest and hugged himself tight, moaning a little, but low, so no one could hear.

A movement in the pattern of shadow and moonshine caught his eye. It was Meg! She'd appeared suddenly out of the darkness on the other side of the road and was climbing the slope beside the dam. Toward the water.

"Go way past the house and out of sight," she'd told him. He'd better do that or she'd get mad again. He set off, the bedrolls bumping awkwardly against his hips, the rope slings sawing into his shoulders. The scratch stung where the dog's fangs had caught his arm, and he grumbled to himself in a low monotonous mutter as he climbed the slope behind the house.

Once over the curve of the hill and out of sight of the house, he made his way back to the track, tossed the bundles over the wire fence, and climbed carefully through after them. It was tougher without Megan to stomp down the lower strands for him.

"Wait," she'd said, so he sat on the bundles and waited.

The night was so still that the feathery glide of a hunting owl startled him nearly out of his wits. He sat bolt upright, his heart thumping loudly, his arms hugging his bony knees. A very long way off a coyote howled at the moon and was echoed by another. And another. Then the silence closed in again. He shivered. Why was she taking so long to fill three canteens? Suppose she didn't come.

That was the thing he was most afraid of. Being alone. Dad was gone, with a hug, the feel of stubble against his cheek, the familiar smell of sweat. Then Mom and the baby cold and stiff in the irrigation ditch. Charlie killed and cut up into steaks. And now Megan. He laid his head on his knees and the stone in his chest grew heavier and heavier.

He had no idea how long he had waited before the silence was broken by a sudden sound. Like thunder, only shorter, without the rumbling echo. A long-ago memory came back. He was small, maybe no more than five, hearing this same sound. Then Dad had come into the yard, laughing, gun slung over his shoulder, two ducks swinging by their feet.

Gunshot? That had been a gunshot! He scrambled to his feet and looked back. The house and outbuildings were out of sight, but a halo of light silhouetted the shape of the slope he had just climbed.

As he hesitated, wondering whether to run back or run away, Megan came into sight at the top of the track. The light was behind her and her shadow ran ahead of her toward him. Quickly he slung the bundles over his shoulders again. Megan slowed down. She zigzagged to and fro across the road as if she couldn't see properly, although by now the moon was higher, making everything as clear as day.

Now she was almost level with him. "Megan, what happened?"

Her face was stony, upturned to the sky, and she didn't even see him. Like he wasn't even there.

"Megan, stop!"

She was passing him now, the canteens in her left hand banging against each other.

"Megan! Megan, stop!"

It was like a horrible nightmare. Like the owl had stolen his soul and he was invisible, a ghost that Megan couldn't see. He looked down at himself, dusty shirt and pants, frayed canvas shoes. *I am here.* He hitched up the bedrolls and began to walk after her as fast as he could. In spite of blinking his eyes tight shut, the tears began again.

"Megan!"

She slowed. Stopped. Turned. He could hardly see

her face, the tears were pouring from his eyes so fast, trickling down his cheeks, inside his nose. He sniffed and ran toward her. "Why didn't you wait? Didn't you hear me? What's the matter?"

Now that she was safely in his sight again and the world had become normal, the fear that had filled him curled up in the shadows inside him, and in its place anger leapt up like fire. He felt like hitting her. Like kicking her shins. Darn girl, scaring him like that. He rubbed his sleeve across his face.

She stood dumbly facing him, her arms hanging limply at her sides, the canteen straps twisted tightly around her left hand. She didn't say a word, but he saw her mouth move.

He stared angrily at her for a long moment, and then he saw it. A ribbon of darkness twisting around her arm like a thin snake, dropping from her fingers to make black spots on the moonlit road.

"Megan, what's that?"

Her mouth opened again and a noise came out like the croak of a thirsty frog. Then slowly, as if someone had cut invisible strings that had been holding her up, she crumpled at his feet. He stared down, saw the dark hole in the back of her arm from which blood was trickling, and his mind began to work.

He dropped the bundles, hunted through one of them for something, anything, that he could use as a bandage. He found a clean sock and fastened it as tightly as he dared and saw, to his relief, the bleeding slow to a stop.

Once he'd done that he tried to straighten her crumpled body. It was heavy. A dead weight. He managed to get a blanket under her head and spread the other over her. He crouched beside her, willing her to open her eyes.

Her face was grave, calm, much older than it looked when she was awake. Her eyelashes made dark crescents against her white cheekbones. She looked like Mom had looked, that last day . . .

◆

"Meg! Meg, please wake up. Don't be dead." Ian was crying, tears splashing hotly on her face.

Numbness at first, and then a sharp pain shooting from shoulder to wrist that made her feel sick. It had been much more comfortable back there in the dark. If she kept her eyes shut she could sink right back . . .

Only, Ian was alone. He was only ten years old. He'd never been anywhere or done anything on his own. He'd never even been to school or known anyone but Mom and Dad. He didn't understand about the badness. He'd never survive on his own.

She forced her eyes open and moved her head a little. That wasn't too bad. She licked her dry lips.

"Water." It was only a croak, but he understood and

held the canteen to her mouth. Some of the precious liquid trickled out of the side of her mouth. Automatically she tried to bring her right hand up to wipe her chin and pain screamed white-hot through her.

"Meg, what are we going to do?"

She found a last scrap of energy inside herself. "Is my arm still bleeding, Ian?"

"No. I managed to stop it. I tied one of my clean socks around it, tight. Is that okay?"

"That was exactly right, Ian."

"You—you're not going to die, too, are you, Meg?"

"No, 'course not. Not now you stopped my arm bleeding. I just feel sick and kind of tired. Remember what it was like the time you fell off the roof? You just slept and slept. I guess I just need to sleep." She looked past Ian, crouching beside her. The moon was just dropping behind the jagged line of the Rockies. The sky was not as dark as it had been. "I must have been out for ages."

"You were." His voice trembled.

"Poor old Ian. Sorry to scare you."

"What are we going to do, then?" He asked again.

"Rest for today. It's nearly dawn. Then we'll go on the way we've been going. With the moon near full we'll be smart to travel at night when it's cool and rest up during the day. That way we'll need less water too."

"There were three canteens. Meg, there's only two."

The misery of her failure swept over Megan again. "I know. I dropped one in the pond when they turned on those lights. Sorry, Ian."

"Heck, we only had two when we started. We're no worse off."

"That's true, isn't it? And we've come more than halfway, I bet."

"Are you hungry, Meg?"

She shook her head and felt her eyes shut. Only thirsty, her body screamed silently, but she wouldn't let herself say the words out loud. Water could cost lives in this dry land. And Ian was so wasteful.

"Be careful of the water," she managed to say.

◆

The pain jolted her awake, a throbbing that seemed to shake her body, as if there were an engine pounding away in her right arm. Beneath the throbbing was a dull ache, like toothache. When she tried to sit up, fire shot through the bone and she bit back a cry.

The sun had risen and the day was already hot. She felt dizzy and sick and, at the sight of Ian chewing on a piece of old gopher meat, her throat filled with bitter bile.

When he saw she was awake he scrambled to his feet and brought her the canteen. She drank the cool water greedily and her nausea faded.

"Something to eat?"

She shook her head, shuddering. "You should have wakened me sooner. The sun's already up."

"You said you needed to sleep today, don't you remember?"

"I did? Maybe we could walk for a bit, till it gets really hot." Megan got slowly to her feet, feeling the road move under her feet. It was like that time, back in first grade, when she'd caught the flu and had to stay home for a whole miserable week. She hadn't been sick since then, not since the school closed down and the neighbors all left. And Ian had never had anything except tummy aches from bad food or water.

She took a deep breath and steadied herself, feet apart on the uncertain road. "Yes, we'd better walk for a little, just to get away from that place. Only I think I'd better have a fresh bandage and maybe a sling. But . . . "

"My spare shirt." Ian ripped one sleeve out, tearing at the fabric with the knife. "You'd better sit down again, Meg."

He undid the sock bandage with slow careful fingers. Megan bit her lip. Every touch, however light, seemed to jolt through her body like a charge of lightning. A clot of blood had stuck the sock to her arm and Ian had to use some of their precious water supply to loosen it. When the sock was off she looked down. Her arm was red and swollen, but she couldn't see any wound.

"Where is it?" She tried to twist her arm.

"Don't. You'll just hurt yourself. It's just a little hole at the back, Meg. It's not bleeding more than a trickle now."

He wrapped the clean cotton shirtsleeve around her arm, tearing the ends up from the cuff and tying them securely. He tore out the second sleeve and put it aside before folding the body of the shirt into a triangle to form a sling.

"How did you ever learn that?"

He grinned proudly. "There were pictures in one of the books Mom had. I used to like looking at the pictures."

The first-aid manual, Megan remembered. It had stood on the shelf above the unused electric stove. *The World Book*, 1998 edition, the Bible, and a few tattered paperbacks. And the first-aid manual, fully illustrated.

The new bandage felt cool and comfortable, and her arm lay heavy and motionless in the sling. "Much better, Ian. Thanks." She managed a smile and didn't tell him what she was thinking, that if there was only one bullet hole in her arm, then the spent bullet was lodged somewhere inside. Sometime it was going to have to come out. What if she got blood poisoning? How long did it take to develop? They used to have drugs a long time ago. She remembered Dad tearing his arm on a bit of barbed wire and Mom worrying about it, putting on hot compresses of chopped herbs—only what herbs? Mom hadn't said, or maybe she'd been too young to remember.

Ian was busily rolling up the bedrolls. He slung one over each shoulder and picked up the canteens.

"Hey, you can't carry all that."

"Sure I can." He staggered off down the road, leaving Meg to follow at her own pace.

Once her feet relearned the rhythm of walking, it wasn't too bad. She had to be careful not to jounce her body or the pain would run up through her arm and she'd feel faint and nauseated again. She let her mind drift and her feet follow each other down the straight dusty road.

She nearly ran into Ian when he stopped to wait for her. "What?"

"It goes uphill here, Meg. Not very much, but . . . well, you *did* say we should rest in the heat and travel at night."

"I did? Good idea. But we need shade."

There was nothing. Beyond the sand-filled ditches the broken fences stretched into the distance, hung with the white skeletons of tumbleweed. Beyond the fence to their right the land rose slightly. To the left it fell away. There was nothing green anywhere. Just spiky clumps of tawny grass and patches of silvery sage.

"I thought maybe we could put one of the blankets in

the ditch and lay the other over the top, maybe with stones to keep it flat. Like a kind of tent?" His voice was diffident, as if he were afraid she'd laugh.

"Sounds great! Can you fix it, Ian?"

"Sure. You just rest."

Megan sank gratefully to the ground and watched in amazement as her small brother bustled about, scooping sand from the ditch with their cooking pot, lining the hollow with one of the blankets.

"C'mon. You lie down and get comfy and I'll put the roof over you."

The shade was like a gift. Enough air drifted in from the lower end to the upper so that, though it was hot, it was not airless. Out of the burning sun this small shade seemed like an oasis.

Megan's eyes closed and she hardly noticed Ian sliding into the shelter, lying sardined to her, his feet against her face. She drifted in and out of sleep, vaguely aware of the small pool of sweat collecting in the hollow of her collarbone, of the throb in her arm that seemed to imitate the rhythm of the grasshopper song outside.

She woke at sunset, feeling Ian crawl cautiously out of their improvised tent. She pushed back the covering blanket and sat up. Ian offered her a slice of gopher meat and she tried to eat it. The emptiness of her stomach hurt, but her mouth was almost too dry to swallow.

She took a swig from her canteen. How light it felt. She shook it. Not much left. She'd have to be more careful. The problem was that her body was crying out for liquid, with all the blood she must have lost. And the sweat. She must have had a bit of fever. But what a waste of water to sweat, she thought ruefully.

Ian folded up the blankets and fastened them into rolls. "Could you carry this canteen?" He casually handed her the other one. It felt heavy, almost full.

"But—"

"It's okay. I don't need as much as you."

She stared at him, really seeing him for the first time since the shooting. His cheeks looked sunken and there were dark circles under his eyes. "Yes, you do. You'll get sick without water. Come on. Take a good drink now, while I'm watching."

He held the bottle to his lips.

"C'mon, Ian. I'm not dumb. Your throat's not moving. Now *swallow*."

He finished drinking, screwed the top down firmly, and handed it back with a sheepish grin. She slung it over her left shoulder and got carefully to her feet. "Okay. Let's get going."

The crimson sunset had faded and the western sky was now a clear pale green, darkening to a deeper blue overhead. The road stretched ahead of them, the land empty and silent on either side. After they had climbed the slight rise, they found the ground falling away ahead of them. They could see for miles, though there was little to see.

The moon rose behind them. The road, which had been ruler straight, now curved in a wide arc to the south around a gentle rise. The line of fence poles stretched ahead, etched starkly in moon shadow.

How unreal the moonlight made the land look, like something out of a dream! The sandy road beneath Megan's feet seemed to ripple like water. It was like walking along a riverbed, a tributary running south-ward and westward to the great river system of the Oldman, the Castle, and the Crowsnest. All that water, rushing down from the mountains . . .

If the water gets much deeper, I'll drown. She felt a new sense of terror and tried to walk tall, taller, keeping her chin up. When she was very small Dad had taught her how to swim in the irrigation canal. She remembered this now and began to make vague swimming gestures with her left arm. It was a pity about her right arm. It wasn't easy swimming left-handed and the canteen got in the way. She slipped it from her shoulder and let it drop to the ground . . . to the bottom of the river. That was better. Now she could really keep her head above the water.

"Megan! Megan!" She could hear his voice, angry. She could hear his feet pounding up the road, back the way they'd just come. It didn't matter. She went on walking . . . swimming . . . downward to the big river where she would find the waterfall . . .

Suddenly she tripped. Ian had dropped the bedrolls in the middle of the road and she fell forward on top of them. She cried out as the pain jolted through her body. She lay there with her eyes shut. When the pain stopped she didn't move. Soft. So soft . . .

Ian was back. "Meg, you dropped your canteen. How *could* you?"

"Not important," she said thickly. "Lots more water out here." She giggled.

"You're not making any sense." He was cross now, with an edge of panic in his voice. "Can you walk some more?"

"Nice here." She snuggled down on the heap of bedrolls.

"But we can't stay out here. . . ." Even through her daze she could hear his panic growing. "We've got to go on. Find more water before morning. Maybe we'll find a good place to stay, people who'll look after you. But there's nothing here."

His innocence stung her back to reality. She struggled into a sitting position. "Don't you go believing that, Ian. You know what it's like. You've seen. Killers with dogs. With guns. Don't you go trusting *nobody*. Promise?"

He mumbled something.

"What? Didn't hear you."

"Okay, okay. I'll do what you say if you'll just get up and walk. I can't carry you *and* the bedrolls."

"No one asked you to." She forced herself to her knees. To her feet. She stood swaying. "Whoops." She giggled.

"I'd help you if I could, Meg." He sounded on the verge of tears.

"I'm just fine. C'mon, crybaby."

She set off down the road. The moon, now over her right shoulder, sent her shadow flickering past the fence posts to her left. It was somehow companionable, this shadow friend. Who was it? Not Dad. That was for sure. Dad hadn't amounted to anything, had he? Just run off and left them when the need was greatest. It was Mom, that's who it was. Mom was with her, letting Megan know that she was doing the right thing, bringing Ian west. In spite of everything that'd gone wrong, it was still the best thing to have done, wasn't it, Mom? To take Ian to the falls. To Uncle Greg.

Water falling, over the edge, down and down, crystal drops caught in the air in a rainbow, shivering on the greenery growing between the clefts of rock. Her left hand went up to the crystal drop around her neck. She stopped dead and fumbled at her collarbone. It was gone. She'd lost it. A promise broken. A lucky charm gone. Now they'd never make it.

"Oh, Mom, Mom," she whispered. "What'll I do?"

But the shadow companion was no longer Mom. It had turned into Mike Spotted Eagle, leading her closer and closer to the buffalo jump. . . . Now it was the guard dog, lips drawn back, hair on the back of its neck stiff like a scrub brush. . . . The man with the gun, bullet-bees buzzing angrily around her. . . .

She broke into a lopsided staggering run, but the shadow enemy was always there, matching stride for stride, no matter how fast she ran. . . .

"Megan! Megan, stop!" It was Ian's voice a very long way off. How had she got so far ahead of him? She tried to warn him of the shadow dangers, but her tongue seemed to have swollen so it filled her whole mouth, and the words wouldn't come out.

◆

The fear uncurled again and became panic. He'd prayed for Megan to come back and she'd come, in spite of the bullets. But she wasn't like the Megan he knew anymore. Strutting down the road talking to herself. She didn't even look like Megan. There was a bright spot of red on each cheek and her eyes were kind of shiny and glazed all at the same time, like there was nobody behind them.

The moon sent thin shadows flickering from the fence posts beside them onto the road, and now and then she'd shy away, like a horse'd shy at shadows, and she'd babble some more, not making any sense. She began to walk slower, waving her left arm around like a crazy woman. As he looked back she stopped and let the precious canteen fall to the ground.

"Megan!" He dropped the bedrolls and ran back along the road for the canteen. When he got back she was lying on her back on the bundles. "Meg, you dropped your canteen. How *could* you?" he asked angrily.

"Not important. Lots more water out here." She giggled and he felt like slapping her face. The panic was shaking his whole body, like a wild animal trying to get out of its cage.

"You're not making any sense. Can you walk some more?"

"Nice here." She snuggled her face against the blanket.

"But we can't stay out here. . . . We've got to go on. . . . There's nothing here." He could feel the tears prickling at his nose again. What was he going to do?

She was on her feet at last, swaying as if the road were moving under her. "Whoops!" she giggled. "C'mon, crybaby."

She was off again on her heedless staggering way,

talking all the time to her invisible companions. She walked faster now. Soon she was running and he couldn't keep up with her.

"Megan, Megan, stop!"

She turned at his voice and, as she had done the night before, suddenly crumpled to the ground.

"Meg! Meg!" But no matter how loudly he called—and he daren't call too loudly in case some bad person should hear—she didn't wake up.

When he was sure that she wasn't going to move, he made her as comfortable as he could with the blankets. He put one of the canteens by her head, so she would see it when she woke up, and he set off down the road alone.

At first he was very frightened, but he found that doing something was much better than doing nothing. As he walked, his short legs covering the ground as fast as they could, he worked out exactly what he would do.

When he eventually reached a farmhouse he approached it cautiously. The roof was solid and the windows were unbroken. No lights showed. The moon had set and the stars were fading, but it'd be a while till the sun came up. They were probably sound asleep. He settled down in the shadow of the gate to watch and listen. The waiting was the hardest part. He kept thinking of Megan lying sick on the road. Suppose she should wake up and wander away. He dug his nails into the palms of his hands and tried not to think of what might happen then.

When at last a rooster broke the silence in a triumphant crow, he could have shouted for joy. He heard the faint bleat of goats and the early morning cluck of hens. He saw smoke trickling from the stovepipe. A screen door slammed somewhere at the back of the building and he saw a shadowy figure plod down the path to the outhouse.

Once the door was safely shut he climbed the gate and tiptoed around the side of the house. When the woman came back she'd find him sitting peacefully on the back steps. He hadn't heard a dog. The figure sure hadn't been carrying a gun. He was only ten years old and maybe they wouldn't be frightened of him. Then he'd have a chance to explain and ask for help. He waited.

◆

"Meg! Meg!" Someone was holding her left arm, shaking it. Later, it seemed, she was being lifted up. Or was she flying? Maybe she'd turned into a bird. There was jolting, not like a bird, that. It hurt and she screamed. Later again, a man's arms were around her. She thought it must be Mike and she was at the cliff edge again. She tried to struggle free and a woman's soft voice broke through her terror.

"There, there. Put the poor bairn down, Mitch." And a soft hand on her hot forehead.

"Mom! Mom, is that you? You're not dead?" Megan's eyes flickered open. She was lying in a shadowy room. Curtains over the window. Three figures bent over her. Who? Ian, of course. Mom? Dad? She'd made it. They were safely home, together again. It had been a bad dream, that's all. Just a horrible dream. She let her eyes close and sank into the softness of a featherbed.

◆

Her arm was a steam engine, shaking her whole body. Burning hot. And huge, like the bolster on Mom and Dad's bed.

"Is that knife clean, Mitch?"

"Yes, Sadie. I boiled it for ten minutes, just like you said."

"Hold her real tight, then."

The pain was monstrous, like an animal tearing her, clawing her apart. She could hear herself screaming, she could feel her legs thrashing, trying to escape from the monster pain.

Then, in the indrawn breath between screams, she heard the small plink of metal dropping on metal.

"There. Bullet's out. I don't think the bone's broke, but it's hard to tell."

"Her arm's real swole up, Sadie."

"Well, of course it is. We'll foment it for now with a good barley poultice. Then you go scrape up some of that mold from the old saddle out back."

"It'll be all dried up by now."

"The goodness'll still be in it. Scrape it on a piece of cloth and we'll wet the cloth and put it against the wound."

The out-of-control shaking of the steam engine had calmed to a slow steady throb. Megan felt the sweaty travel-stained clothes being peeled off her body. A wet cloth was rubbed over her hot skin. A sheet covered her, cool, smooth, scented with sage-wind. She sighed and felt herself drift away. But there was something she had to do first. . . .

"Ian?" She opened her eyes, frowning. Looking for him.

"I'm here, Meg. Everything's okay. Honest it is."

How can everything be all right? she worried. We're among strangers. "I told you . . . *strangers* . . . don't trust . . ."

SEVEN

Strangers, Megan had called them, warning him. Funny, thought Ian, shoveling fried eggs and barley cakes into his mouth. He felt that he'd known Sadie and Mitch all his life. Specially Mitch. Mitch made him feel like a *man*.

"What're we going to do today, Mitch?"

The old man pushed his sweat-stained hat back, exposing his freckled forehead. "Well," he drawled, "I've been thinking for a while I'd like to build a stronger henhouse. Them coyotes are getting sassier every night. I've seen their prints right across the yard.

But it's a job for two. D'you feel like lending a hand?"

"You bet." Ian gulped his glass of goat's milk and used the last of his bread to mop up the egg yolk and grease off his plate. It was great eating real food again. Sadie knew what a guy needed. Not like Megan, feeding him gopher meat and berries and weeds. Ever since they'd arrived, Sadie'd stuffed him with food three times a day, not counting snacks between whiles. He could see the difference already, the way his ribs didn't stick out anymore. And he was getting muscles in his arms. Real muscles.

"Ready to go."

"Don't forget your hat." Sadie turned from the sink to beam at him.

"No, ma'am." He jammed it on his head and swaggered outdoors after Mitch.

All morning he held planks steady while Mitch sawed, and passed him nails when he hammered. The sweat trickled into his eyes and his legs ached, but he didn't give in, not till Mitch said it was too hot to work anymore. In the afternoon they rested indoors, Sadie and Mitch snoring in their armchairs, while he wandered around the living room, looking at the bits of china and glass that had belonged to Sadie's grandmother. After a snack they worked some more. In two days the new henhouse was finished, so solid, Mitch said, that it'd take a charging buffalo to dislodge it.

"Couldn't have done it without you, boy."

It was better than any thanks.

"What d'you want me to help you with next, Mitch?"

"Well . . ." Mitch made as if to push his hat back, only he was in the house when Ian asked him, so he wasn't wearing it. He'd still make the gesture, though, and look surprised that there was nothing in the way of his hand. "Well, maybe we could work on a better pen for the goats. I tell you, them coyotes . . ."

It wasn't all work, though. In the late summer evenings, when the sun was setting bloody red behind the Rockies to their left, they sat on the porch, looking north over the softly rolling land that had once been Mitch and Sadie's cattle ranch. Sadie would rock and mend while Mitch taught Ian how to whittle. There wasn't a lot of wood to whittle with, but Mitch cut willow branches from the creek and showed Ian how to sharpen a knife and the right way to hold it so he wouldn't cut himself even if it slipped. Before long, Ian had made a whistle all by himself that really worked, shrill enough to call Charlie from gopher-hunting. If only Charlie . . .

He ran in to Megan, still recovering in the spare room bed, and gave her a blast on it. "Ouch!" She put her good hand over her ear and buried the other in her pillow. "That's plenty loud."

"Mitch is going to learn me some tunes. Wait till you hear them."

"I'm in no hurry." She grinned at him, almost in her old way. The fever-flush had gone from her face, and now she looked pale and kind of tired. "You behaving yourself?"

"Sure. I'm helping. Mitch says he couldn't do without me."

She frowned at that. "He's going to have to. Soon as I'm up and about we've got to be on our way."

"But—"

"No buts. You know we can't stay forever. We've got to get to Uncle Greg's."

Uncle Greg. She was always on about him, like getting there was the most important thing in the whole world. And she didn't even know what Uncle Greg was like. Maybe he was mean. Maybe he wouldn't want them. While Mitch . . . He wandered back into the kitchen. Mitch was in the big rocker, fanning himself with his old hat. Sadie stood by the woodstove, cooking something whose smell wandered across the room, into his nose, and down to his stomach. His mouth watered. He sure was hungry.

Leave. Why'd Megan want to talk about leaving? He pushed the worry from his mind and settled on the old hearth rug by Mitch's leg, resting his head against Mitch's knee, comforted by the familiar man-smell of sweat and garden dirt. I'm never going to leave here, he told himself. Never.

♦

Alone in the small spare room, with its white curtains and white cotton bedspread, Megan turned her head restlessly. She had to get better fast, get on her way. How hot it was.

Sadie bustled in, smiling, with cool water to bathe her hot body, and chicken soup to nourish her back to strength. Beyond the room she seemed to hear always the shrill voice of Ian and the low rumbled replies of Mitch. She'd only seen Mitch the once, when he'd hovered in the door, battered hat in hand, and told her, "Now, you hurry up and get well. Don't fret about the boy. I'll see he comes to no harm."

Like Sadie, he was leather-skinned, the sandy color of the soil, hands and arms blotched with dark spots. Mitch's hair was thin, though, while Sadie's was still thick, pure white, pulled back into a stiff knot at the back of her neck.

Don't fret, he'd said. But how could she not? She'd gone and got herself shot and stuck in bed, while Ian ran around the place, eating them out of house and home, she'd bet, and the days went by, getting them no closer to Lundbreck and Uncle Greg. She'd even gone and lost her lucky crystal.

"You've been awful kind," she said to Sadie. "I don't

know how we'll pay you back. We don't even have the hens anymore."

"Let's have no talk of paying back. It's only neighborly. Like the good Samaritan picking up the wounded man from the roadside and carrying him to the inn and looking after him. It's no more than a person's duty."

"Those others didn't think like that, Sadie."

"Them survivalists?" Sadie snorted. "I call them 'firstists.' Meaning they don't believe in the good Lord, only in being first, grabbing the food and water and letting the rest of the world go hang. Badly raised as children, I reckon."

"Why would they stay here instead of going on to the coast?"

"They say the coast's in a bad mess, too, what with the floods and all. Funny, isn't it? We don't have a drop of water from one year's end to the next and there they are with too much of it and the sea level rising every year. But those crazy survivalists, they're still more scared of the bomb than they are of the weather. I guess they figure they'll be safer out here where there's not too many folks to bother them. Now, are you comfy?"

"Yes, thank you, Sadie."

"Then I'll leave you to have another sleep."

"Sadie?"

"Yes, m'dear?"

"When'll I be well enough to travel?"

"Now, we'll worry about that when the time comes. Right now what you need is rest."

◆

Rest. It seemed to Megan that all she did was sleep and eat. Her legs got fidgety and she begged to be allowed to get up. Sitting in a bentwood rocker in the kitchen, with her arm in a sling, was certainly better than counting the cracks in the ceiling of the spare bedroom, though not quite what Megan had had in mind.

"Mitch says all the spread up north there, as far as you can see, used to belong to him and Sadie," Ian told her.

"Still does, I suppose." Mitch's hand went to his forehead as if to push back his hat. "We raised beef cattle and irrigated all that bottomland for hay."

"It was a good life, back then, what with the children—six of them we had, four boys and two girls," Sadie chimed in. "But even then they chose the cities rather than stay and farm. All except for Dinny. He bought himself a place in the Okanagan, did all right there, and his eldest son took over, I hear. But we've not had news of any of them in a long while."

"That's awful." Megan remembered with sudden pain the long winter before the baby had come, waiting for Dad to return or at least for a message, a letter, brought by a passing traveler. And she saw reflected in Sadie's eyes the look that had been in Mom's as the days had gone by and the darkness of January and the howling wind had driven them all near crazy.

"Ain't no way of getting mail out here," Mitch put in. "Last we heard, from a couple traveling east with a letter they dropped off for us, Dinny was asking us to go out to British Columbia and settle down there in some kind of old folks' home."

"But that was about ten years ago and we didn't feel the need, did we, Mitch?"

"And don't now. We got a spring still runs. And there's the goats and hens keep us fed. And the wife's vegetable garden. We're all right here. The secret's you've got to learn to take only what you need from the land and give back what it's given you. Respect. That's all. That's what you've got to have for the land. Respect."

"What d'you mean, Mitch? The land's just there, ain't it?" Ian looked happy, happier than he'd looked in years, snuggled up against Mitch's bony knees, and Megan felt a little twinge. She'd done everything she could for him, but it was this man who was the more important now. She pushed the horrid jealousy out of her mind and tried to pay attention to the conversation.

Mitch was shaking his head. He pushed his invisible hat back on his forehead once more. "The rivers'll run forever, eh? That's what the natives used to think. Then we come along and dam them, the Oldman, the Crowsnest, the Castle. Meddling with nature. More water for irrigation. More hay. More beets. More cattle. Then you got to have more irrigation. Pretty soon all the fertilizer that's settled in the soil starts to come up to the surface again—"

"Like a forgotten sin," Sadie put in. "Like the mark of Cain."

"We saw alkali on the way from the Porcupine Hills," Megan put in.

"There you are, then. Some of that's just natural, farther east, I heard tell. But the rest we brung on ourselves. Greed and grab. That's what done it. And not for the first time."

"Like in the Depression, you mean?" Megan asked. "I remember in the old days, when the weather started getting real bad, people used to talk about the weather being like their grandparents said it was in the Depression."

"I'm thinking further back than that. Thousands and thousands of years ago. I read it in one of my books. There was a place that they say grew the best wheat in the world. It was stuck between two rivers, the Tigris and the Eu-phrate-ees, like it might be here, between the Oldman and the Crowsnest, say. Back then the priests used to look after things—"

"Like it might be the government," Sadie interrupted.

"And they watched the stars and told the farmers when to plant, and they let the water into the irrigation canals at the proper time like they'd learned from the priests before them. And it was all orderly, see?"

"What went wrong, then?" Megan asked.

"I reckon what happened was that people got to thinking, If I took a bit more water later on I could get two crops. It was wonderful sunny in that country, like it is up here. So they stopped paying attention to the priests and irrigated their land twice a year. So then the salt started coming up and pretty soon they couldn't grow wheat anymore and they had to turn to barley. Barley'll grow in land that salty, wheat won't tolerate it. But after a while barley wouldn't grow either. And the land dried up and the wind blew and today it's nothing but sand."

"Like here."

"Like here's getting, if we don't try to save it."

"Isn't it too late, Mitch?" Megan asked. "Everyone's left. Except for those survivalists we didn't see nobody on the road."

"Good thing for the land they've gone. No more greedy grabbing. Maybe she'll heal if we leave her in peace."

I wonder, thought Megan. The wind blows and it doesn't rain. Can it heal?

That night Megan lay in her featherbed, staring at the ceiling. The curtains blew in and out and the light from the waning moon danced patterns of light and shade around the room. The buffalo, she remembered, had grazed the prairies in their millions and the grassland had sustained them. It hadn't blown away. The grasshoppers hadn't flown through in black clouds to destroy it. So what had gone wrong when white people had come west?

Mitch had talked about the early settlers breaking the land to wheat. Maybe that word was truer than they'd reckoned. Maybe *breaking* the land was just what they'd done. Broken and broken it. Till there wasn't enough strength left in the land to heal what had been broken. Maybe the land was dying and nothing could save it.

"Ian, are you asleep?"

"Uh-huh."

"D'you remember a time when the land was different?"

"Huh? How different?"

"From now. Sand and sage and tumbleweed."

"That's the way land is, i'n'it?" His voice trailed off sleepily.

Megan stared at the ceiling.

◆

Three days later the bandage came off and there were

just two ugly puckered scars on Megan's arm to remind her of the encounter with the survivalists.

"You've been wonderful and I'll never forget your kindness," she said to Sadie. "But we should be on our way."

"Where's your hurry? While there's breath in my body I'll look after the stranger in need. And Mitch feels the same, praise the Lord."

"Thank you. It's just . . . we're eating your food, using your water. You've got enough for yourselves. But with two extra, that's twice as much water. Twice as much food. More, when you think of Ian's appetite."

"Bless the boy. He's got a hollow leg, hasn't he just? It's a pleasure to watch him. Needs fattening up. I don't mean to criticize, me dear, but he's right undernourished."

Megan felt herself flushing. "I know. But toward the end there wasn't any more. We were eating gophers and weeds and that was about it."

"Lord save us! No wonder the boy's skin and bone."

"You've got the garden now, and the hens are laying. But come winter . . . we must go before then."

"I dunno." Saddie shook her head. "Mitch is getting right fond of that boy. The two of them are out there this minute, cleaning up the creek."

"I hope Ian's wearing his hat." Megan frowned. She

still felt mixed up inside at the way Ian had taken to Mitch.

"Bless your heart, Mitch won't let the boy come to any harm, you can be sure of that. Though how having no ozone up there is dangerous when they say it's a poisonous gas is more than I can figure. Now, would you like to go collect the eggs for me?"

Outside, in the quivering heat, Megan squinted her eyes and looked about her. She felt pale and shut in. Whether there was a hole in the sky or not, the sun's rays were a pleasant change. She carefully unhooked the door to the new chicken run. It had a slatted roof, so that the sunlight barred the ground in even stripes.

Back in the house with her basketful of eggs, Meg took a candle and went carefully down the rough wooden stairs into the cellar beneath the kitchen. It was amazingly cool down here, the dirt floor smelling clean and damp. She held up her candle and looked around.

There were bins of sand where Sadie must store potatoes, carrots, and turnips for the winter, and there were shelves along the left wall where she must have kept preserves. Now the glass sealers were empty and dust-filmed. On the ceiling there were large hooks, but only a single braid of withering onions hung from them.

Along the back wall Mitch had fashioned a stone shelf, and here Sadie kept her milk, butter, cheese, and eggs. There was one egg in the dish. Megan set it to one side and put in the eight eggs she had gathered today. Nine eggs altogether. What would happen come winter, she wondered, when the days were dark and cold and the hens stopped laying?

There was a bucket of stuff for preserving eggs on the dirt floor—Mom had had one just like it—but there were not many eggs, barely enough to cover the bottom. She and Ian had been given a couple of eggs for their breakfast every day—more if they asked, and Ian always asked.

She bit her lip and looked around the cellar once more. Then she climbed the stairs carefully, blew out the candle, and took the basket up the creekside to pick fodder for the goats. "They'll eat everything down to the roots if we let them run loose," Sadie said. "And then there's those pesky coyotes." So the goats were tethered in the shade and were hand-fed on the growing tips of the bushes along the creek to keep them healthy and producing lots of milk for butter and cheese. But did they produce enough for two extra hungry mouths?

◆

When the creek had been cleared, Ian helped Mitch haul water to the vegetable garden. Cleaning up the creek had been fun, ankle-deep in the cool water, his jeans rolled up to his knees. They'd shored up a weak bank with stones and thrown out sticks and decayed vegetation that had washed down. But hauling water was no fun at all.

"Why don't we dig a channel from the creek? It'd be a heck of a lot easier."

"Well now, it's like this." Mitch straightened up and pushed his sweat-stained hat off his forehead. "If we was to do that, the sun'd suck the water outer the channel and the dry dirt'd suck it down. We'd lose more water one way 'n the other. Now, pouring it around the roots here, it's tedious, I'll allow, but you don't waste a drop."

"But it takes so long!"

"Where's your hurry, boy? We've got a whole day ahead of us."

Ian thought about this as he staggered up the rise from the creek with yet another pailful, careful not to spill a drop. "But you've got channels dug to your barley field, ain't you?"

"Sure. I open them in the spring, when the creek's high with snow-melt, and I let enough through just to get the shoots started. Barley's important to us, son. Gives us bread and porridge, grain for the chicks, and the chopped-up straw's handy for the goats. So I use water just to get it started. After that it's on its own. 'Course, sometimes it rains." He looked up pensively at the cloudless sky, his long skinny throat rising like a chicken's neck from his cotton shirt.

"Really? Rain?" Ian stood by Mitch, hands on his hips like the old man's, staring at the sky.

"Someday soon, I shouldn't wonder."

◆

The rain came three days later and they all ran out and stood in the yard with the rain soaking through their clothes. The ground darkened as the large drops landed. The chickens ran to and fro, frisking up their feathers, and a little precious rain trickled off the sloping roof into the covered rain barrel.

In ten minutes the downpour was over. "There's more clouds over there." Ian pointed.

Mitch squinted up and shook his head. "Just empties coming back," he sighed.

"Never heard that before. What's it mean, Mitch?" Ian stopped dancing around the yard and stared up at Mitch with that devoted look in his eyes that was beginning to get on Megan's nerves.

"That's what our folks used to say back in the 1930s, back in the last bad times. To everyone else it was the Great Depression, but to us on the prairies it was the Dirty Thirties. They'd see the grain cars going by on the railroad line, past all the little towns with their high proud elevators full of nothing but promises, so the grain cars'd have to go back empty to the lakehead.

'Empties coming back,' folks'd say. A year's sweat, a year's hope, another year of going without. And the clouds were the same, d'you see? Nothing in them but false promises."

◆

When Megan had been very sick, Ian had slept on the couch in the parlor. Now he had a truckle bed next to hers in the spare room. That night Megan sat up in bed, after Sadie had kissed them good night and reminded them to say their prayers. She relit the candle by her bed. "We've got to talk."

"What about? I'm sleepy. It's a lot of work cleaning out the creek and hauling water, you know, Meg. Mitch says—"

"Yeah, I'm sure. But listen up, Ian. We've got to think about moving on."

"Let's not go."

"There's not that many bean bushes in the vegetable patch, Ian. Nor hens or goats either. Enough for *them*. Two old people with small appetites. I've been down in the root cellar and looked round. There's not a speck left over from last year. I reckon they've managed so that they have just enough to get through each winter and into the following summer, but they sure don't have enough for two more people. Especially when one of us is a growing boy with a hollow leg—that's what Sadie calls it."

"I'll be helping Mitch. He says I'm as good as an extra hand already. When I've growed a bit he says—"

"It's next winter I'm worried about. We're eating into their stores. Ian, we've got to go on, find our own place. Make our own way."

The room was silent. Outside a coyote howled. Megan shivered at the lonely sound.

"Are you listening to me, Ian?"

"Uh-huh."

She blew out the light and lay watching the shadows of moon and windblown curtain on the ceiling. In the darkness she heard Ian sniff.

"What's the matter?"

"I don't want to go."

"I do understand, Ian."

"No, you don't." His whisper was fiercely angry. "You don't understand a bit. Mitch, he's like Dad was, only better. He makes me feel I'm important. He couldn't have finished the henhouse without me helping, he said. And we're planning a new pen for the goats. I've never been of any account to anyone, not in my whole life. Just a ten-year-old nuisance-kid. That's all. With Mitch it's different."

"You *are* of account, Ian Dougal. You always have been. You know how much you meant to Mom. And me. . . . I know I get a bit impatient sometimes, but that don't mean anything."

"But I *love* Mitch."

There. It was out. The thing that had been eating at Megan was in the open at last. Look after your brother, Mom had said before she died. And she'd promised. She'd worried. She'd planned. She'd tried to do the right thing. And the first half-decent person they meet Ian cosies up to like he never had a family of his own worrying, planning, caring about him. I love Mitch, he says.

The silence stretched on. Megan took a deep breath. "Okay. I do understand. But if you really love him, you're going to have to think of his future as well as yours. There's not enough food and water for all of us, and that's the truth. Think about it. Okay?"

Then she firmly turned on her side, away from the moonlight, and buried her head in her pillow.

EIGHT

Ian woke early with the feeling that something was wrong. The sun sent a line of brightness between the drapes onto the opposite wall, and he could hear the chooks clucking lazily outside. He stretched and felt good. Then he remembered Megan's plan. He slid quietly out of bed, put on his jeans and shirt, and dabbed his face with water from the basin on the dresser. He tiptoed to the door. Megan sighed and turned over and he froze, hand on the knob. He waited until he heard her regular breathing before sliding through and pulling the door shut after him.

"My, but you're up early. Did you wash your face?"

"Yes, ma'am."

"Then come here and let me fix your hair." She flattened it down with a brush from the big old dresser against the kitchen wall. "There. That's better."

She kissed the top of his head and Ian put his arms around her waist and hugged her, the clean sun-dried cotton of her dress against his face.

"My, what's that for?"

"Nothing special. Where's Mitch?"

"Out back. Fixing something."

"I'll give him a hand." Ian was out the door in a flash.

"Don't forget your hat! Well, bless the boy, the sun's barely up. He'll be all right."

Her voice came faintly to Ian, but he didn't heed it. "Mitch, Mitch, you there?"

He bounded through the vegetable garden to the edge of the field where Mitch stood, an ear of barley in his hand. "Watcha doing, Mitch?"

"Checking if this here grain's ripe enough. We get some fierce winds through the gap over yon. I'd like to cut afore the next blow."

"I can help with the cutting and threshing. You'll need all the hands you can get, I bet."

"Well, now . . ." Mitch pushed his hat back and looked down at Ian. His blue eyes were filmed with age, Ian noticed, like the whites of eggs just before they set, and the rims were red with dust and sun, but they still had a twinkle in them. "Well now, you offering to become a permanent hand around the place?"

Ian nodded vigorously.

"By rights you should be in school."

"Ain't never been to school."

Mitch tutted. "Well, maybe in Lundbreck—that's where you're aiming for, ain't it?—maybe there's a school there."

"I don't want to go. Let me stay here, Mitch." He butted his head against the old man's chest, smelling his sweat, hearing the steady thump of his heart through the boniness, feeling the big hand ruffle his hair. "Don't make me go."

"I've grown right fond of you, son, that's certain. Don't worry your head about it. We'll just go on the way we're going and see how things turn out."

Megan'll go on at you, Ian wanted to warn him. She'll make the going sound right and proper. But it ain't. It *ain't*.

Sure enough, once breakfast was on the table—fried barley cakes, but only one egg today, Ian noticed regretfully—Megan began. "We have to leave, Sadie. You've been real good to us. Well, you saved our lives, I guess, specially mine. And . . ." Her voice wobbled and got steady again. "And you've treated us like family."

"You've been like family, my dears."

"Mitch wants me to stay on," Ian interrupted. Lucky I got up early, he thought, and said my say first. "I'm going to help with harvesting the barley. There's a lot to do, what with cutting and threshing and—"

"Winnowing," Mitch put in. "I reckon I could use an extra hand, Sadie."

"What do *you* know about harvesting, Ian Dougal?" Megan glared at him. "It was a poultry farm we had and you never did a stroke of work there, I recall." She turned to Mitch. "He's only a little boy. Not like a man, to really earn his keep. And he eats as much as the two of you put together."

"He needs fattening up, that's for sure." Sadie nodded.

"Don't talk about me like I'm not here, all of you," Ian yelled. "I wanna stay and Mitch wants me to too. If you're so crazy about finding Uncle Greg, well, why don't you just go on by yourself, Megan Dougal?"

"Oh, I don't know about that . . ."

"Now, let's not be hasty . . ."

The two old people spoke in chorus, and looked at each other in dismay.

"You know I can't just leave you, Ian. I'm in *charge*."

"I'm sick of you bossing me around. I want Mitch."

"What d'you think, Sadie?" Mitch pushed his hand up onto his forehead in the familiar gesture.

"Well . . ."

Megan looked at Sadie and then down at Sadie's plate. She'd gone without an egg and taken only a single slice of barley bread. "We *have* to go," she said quietly. "You know, you understand."

Sadie sighed and nodded. "It's for the best, Mitch, believe me."

Ian pushed his chair back violently, scraping the floor. "I hate you! I hate all of you, but specially you, Megan Dougal." He ran outdoors, letting the screen door slam behind him.

"Maybe I'd better—" Mitch got to his feet.

"Let him cool off a mite first, Mitch. He's too mad to listen right now. Why don't you make a map to show the young'uns the best way of getting to Lundbreck from here? I'll get the stove hot for some baking. They'll need food for the road."

"We've taken so much already. You don't have to—"

"No one leaves this house empty-handed, my girl. Gophers and weeds indeed! Only fit for heathens. How long'll it take them, Mitch?"

"Less than two days, I'd say, Sadie."

"Then I'll give them food for three, just to be on the safe side. The paper you want's in the dresser there, by the way."

Mitch sat at the table with a sheet of yellowing paper and a stub of pencil and began to work. "I'm not much of a hand at drawing, but getting to Lundbreck's about like this here."

Megan watched over his shoulder, noticing the thinning hair, the scrawny neck and shoulders. He looked frail. "Why don't you come too? Sadie, what d'you think? Would you? Maybe you wouldn't have to work so hard. We'd look after you, honest."

"I don't know as how I could bear to leave all this." Sadie looked around the tidy kitchen and through the window to the vegetable patch, the field, and the barren hills beyond. "I don't think I could, my dear. The creek still runs good and the Lord has preserved our health. But there is something you can do for me."

"Sure, Sadie. Anything."

"Take a letter for my son with you as far as Lundbreck, and then when you're settled, see if you can send it along with someone going past Peachland."

"Of course I will."

"And if you don't like it at Lundbreck—if anything's happened to your uncle, anything like that—you know you're right welcome back here."

"Oh, Sadie . . ."

"Now, I'd best get my baking done and my letter writ. You'll be going tomorrow morning, I expect?"

"First thing, before it gets hot."

"And I'd best talk to that young man. He should have

cooled off by now." Mitch got to his feet with a grunt. "You got that map safely stowed away?"

Megan patted her skirt pocket and he went out.

"I feel right bad at letting you young'uns go," Sadie said quietly after the screen door had snapped shut behind him.

"Please don't. You've been great. And it's not just that you don't have enough to feed us, Sadie. He needs kids his own age. He needs school. But I'll miss you something awful."

◆

Mitch found Ian face down under the wolf willows that edged the creek. He sat down beside him and patted his shoulder awkwardly. A hawk slowly circled a thermal against the hills to the north. Mitch watched it silently. After a while Ian rolled over and sat up. Mitch dropped a bony arm over his shoulder and they sat quietly watching the hawk. It dived suddenly to the ground and rose again.

"There goes a ground squirrel, I guess."

"Wish I was free. Like that bird. Not made to go places. By a *girl*." Ian glanced up at Mitch.

Mitch rubbed a hand over his stubbly chin. "Don't know as how the hawk's that free. I know it looks that way. But he flies 'cause he's hungry, 'cause that's the only way he's going to get to eat. And he can't go any place he fancies. He's got to follow where the wind goes, d'you see?"

"Yeah," said Ian reluctantly, and they were silent again.

"D'you ever fish in this creek, Mitch?" he asked at last. He wiped his nose on his sleeve.

"Nah. Nothing worth catching anymore. Used to be."

"Will there be any fishing over that way?" He jerked his head westward.

"I'm sure of it. Up where the water's still cold and clean. Tell you what, son. I've got an old rod and reel in the shed back of the house just a-gathering dust. Would you like to take it with you? Maybe you'll even catch something on the way."

"Wow! Will you really?" Ian managed a watery smile. "That'll sure surprise Megan."

"Let's go dig it out right now." Mitch unwound his long body and hauled Ian to his feet. They walked back to the house in companionable silence.

◆

Megan woke very early, before sunup, and shook Ian awake. Sadie was already in the kitchen, cooking breakfast for them. They ate silently and, when their last meal together was over, Megan filled their canteens.

Sadie handed her the bundles of food she had prepared, wrapped in clean cloth, and Megan tucked them securely into her bedroll, hoisted it to her shoulder, and slung the canteen after it with a grimace. Her right arm was still very stiff and the muscle had shrunk from lack of use and still gave a tweak of pain now and then. But I'm in pretty good shape, she told herself. And Ian's never looked better. She looked at him, wrestling with the knots of his own bedroll. His cheeks had filled in and he was almost chubby, the peaky fledgling look completely gone.

She hesitated by the door, wanting to get this last painful moment over. It was like the bandages on her arm. There were two ways of getting them off. You could pull real fast, with a moment's agony. Or you could soak it and peel it, bit by bit, knowing that in the end there was still going to be an instant when it would hurt like crazy.

Sadie helped her. "Here's the letter for my son. Put it in a safe place. Land's sakes, you're not thinking of setting off without a hat?"

"But I don't have one, remember? I've been borrowing yours."

"No point in addling your brains." Sadie lifted the battered straw off the peg by the door. She plopped it on Megan's head and gave her a hearty kiss on both cheeks.

"There. Now off with you both. And God bless."

"Good-bye, Sadie. Good-bye, Mitch. Thank you for everything. I'll make sure your letter goes on. And we *will* be back to see how you're doing. C'mon, Ian."

She turned away and walked resolutely through the door into the heat. It's worse for him. He needs a man and he missed Dad more'n I did, I guess.

She walked west along the trail until, as Mitch's sketch map showed, it met an all-weather road running north and south. She dropped her load and squatted at the roadside to wait for Ian. Gentle hills hid the distant view. The sage was silver green, small stunted bushes. Spikes of dry grass held the blowing dust. The sky was as blue as ever, a few very small clouds scudding by on the westerly wind. Empties going back, Mitch had called them.

Only strong people could survive in this land, she thought. But there's two ways of being strong, isn't there? There's strong with guns and dogs, like those survivalists. And then there's strong like Mitch and Sadie. Will Uncle Greg be like Mitch? Or like the others?

She looked east along the trail. There was Ian at last, kicking up a cloud of yellow dust as he scuffed his feet reluctantly along the road. She looked down at her own shoes. The canvas uppers had split along the sides and the toe caps were beginning to peel away. The soles had worn as smooth as glass. When she walked over pebbly ground she could feel every stone against the bottom of her feet. Would they have shoes at Lundbreck? And how was she going to pay for them?

When Ian caught up with her she got up, grimacing at the unexpected stiffness in knees and thighs. She swung her bundle to her shoulder and gave Ian a welcoming grin, pretending not to notice his red eyes and blotchy face.

"You didn't have to wait. I'd have caught up."

"That's okay. We don't follow the road, according to Mitch's map. We've got to go that way, cross-country." She pointed west. "It won't be bad. Less'n a mile before we hit the trail again. Got all your stuff okay?"

"Yeah."

"Here goes, then." Her cheerful voice sounded false in her ears. She stomped down the strands of barbed wire for Ian to climb through.

The going was more difficult now. There were tussocks of harsh grass to avoid, the twisting roots of sagebrush and the holes of ground squirrels to watch out for. But it was also more interesting than plodding along a road. They crossed a dry creekbed and the land rose again on the far side.

Even a gentle hill like this made Megan's legs ache. Strolling around the farm, even up the creek for fodder, as she recovered from her wound was poor preparation for a cross-country hike.

The trail, unmarked, unfenced, almost hidden by

blown sand, appeared on their right shortly after they climbed up from the creek bottom. Reassuringly it led them westward, toward the still hidden mountains.

They mounted a slight rise and there, like a green snake flung across the sandy land, was the wriggling shape of the Oldman River, the tiny beginnings of the same river Megan had seen from the lookout on the Porcupine Hills. On its far side was a wide sandy plain, and beyond it rose majestically the toothed line of the Rockies. Somewhere across that river was their destination.

Megan smoothed out the map. "Look, Ian. It really isn't far now. We've almost made it."

He didn't answer her or look at the map. His face was no longer red and puffy, but under the shade of his cotton hat it had a closed, wary look. Megan fought back the irritation that his sulks always brought on. After all, she argued with herself, he's lost Dad and Mom, Charlie, and now Mitch. Can't blame him.

But what about *me*, a small voice whined. I lost Mom and Dad too. And Sadie. Though I guess we weren't quite as close as Mitch and Ian. Or in a different way. We both understood what empty pantry shelves meant.

"C'mon, then. We'll go down to the river. Have a good drink and rest till early evening. There's a road on the far side, so we can walk right on until it gets dark."

Their trail ended abruptly, as if it had been wiped out with an eraser. There was no sign of the farmhouse to which it must have originally led. Down the cleared slope a few new seedlings of wolf willow and saskatoon withered in the heat. At the bottom the river meandered between sandbanks.

"There used to be a dam along here, Mitch said. The water was once backed up right to the top of the ravine. Imagine, all this valley being full of water."

Ian shook his head. "Where'd the water go?"

"I guess once it got real dry they needed the water downstream and had to let it out."

"Lucky they did or we'd have to swim across. And I can't swim."

"There's a bit more shade on this side, Ian. Let's rest here. I'm beat." Megan let the bedroll fall from her shoulder with a sigh of relief. She dropped onto the slope, her head on the bedroll, Sadie's old straw hat over her face. The sand burned through her back.

"I guess it's okay to have a drink?"

"Sure. There's a whole river down there." Her voice dragged sleepily. Her eyes shut. Just a little nap'd be okay . . .

◆

The sun was shining directly into her eyes. It was over the mountains. She woke with a start and sat up. Ian's bedroll was close by but he was nowhere in sight.

"Ian!" She scrambled to her feet, her heart pounding, and stared around.

It was all right. There he was, down close to the water. She yelled again and he turned and waved and came scrambling up the steep sides of the coulee toward her.

"What were you doing down there?"

"Fishing."

"How?"

"Mitch gave me a rod. It works pretty good."

"Did you catch anything? Some fresh fish'd be nice for a change."

"Yeah, but they're no good." His voice was disgusted. "When I went to gut them they was all wormy."

"Guess the water's too warm for them. Not healthy."

"Mitch says that where we're going the water'll be cold. Maybe I'll catch good fish there, eh, Meg? Say, can we look at what Sadie's packed, huh? There's lots. I saw. Enough for lunch as well as supper."

"More like a tea party," said Megan, suddenly remembering a long-ago ritual of boiled eggs and biscuits with butter and chokecherry jam.

Ian squatted on the slope below Megan and threw his hat aside. The wind lifted his fine pinky-blond hair. She ruffled it with her fingers. It was damp with sweat. "You put that hat back on, d'you hear?"

"Yes, ma'am," he answered with an impudent grin. But he did put his hat back on.

There actually were hard-boiled eggs in the bundle,

and they ate them with buttered barley bread and all the water they could drink. Then, at the water's edge, they refilled the canteens.

"Take off your shoes and socks before you wade across," Megan warned. "If you walk far in wet shoes you'll get blisters."

"Yes, ma'am."

"What's all this 'ma'am' business? You're driving me crazy."

"Mitch said I was to treat you respectful and mind what you say."

"That's good. But Meg'll do me fine."

They crossed the river from sandbank to sandbank. At its deepest the water was no more than up to Ian's knees. And warm. Slow moving. In the shadows fish moved languidly as if dazed. No wonder Ian had been able to catch them so easily.

They rubbed their feet dry and put back their shoes and socks. Once out of the ravine on the western side, they could see clearly the devastation of the land. What must at one time have been a broad fertile plain was now a wind-scoured desert upon which nothing grew, from the foothills in the west to the gentle slopes to the north.

It was worse than anything they had seen since they had left the farm. Always there had been a little sage and speargrass, the remains of Russian thistle in the skeleton structures of tumbleweed. Here there was nothing at all.

"Why is it so awful?" Megan gasped.

"Mitch said . . ."

In spite of her dismay at the destroyed land ahead of them, Megan couldn't help smiling at Ian's phrase. I'd better get used to it, she thought wryly. I guess there's going to be a lot of it, for a while anyway.

"Mitch said that this was all irrigated. Some of the best wheat land in the west, he said."

The broken, wounded land, Megan thought. This is what death looks like. She shivered. "C'mon. Let's find that road and get outa here."

Though there were no holes or sagebrush roots to look out for, the going was not easy. Sometimes the sand was wind-packed and as hard as a road. At other times it suddenly became soft, yielding, and their shoes sank deeply as if into mud.

Ian had regained his spirits, and he certainly had a lot more energy than Megan. She was content to let him run ahead while she plodded along, concentrating on lifting up each tired leg and putting it down again. Her bedroll seemed to get heavier by the minute, but she could no longer change shoulders as she would have done before her injury. Though the wound had healed enough not to need a bandage, Sadie had warned her not to overuse it. The twinge of pain, when she tried to swing her load to her other shoulder, was enough to remind her.

"Hey, look, Megan. Isn't this weird?"

Ian was standing beside a swirling line of sand, somehow different in texture from the rest of the plain. "What made it this way, d'you reckon?"

"I dunno. Looks kind of like a river, doesn't it? A river of sand instead of water."

The possibility of what her words might mean clicked into her mind just as Ian ran forward. "No, don't. Not that way. It could be . . ." She ran after him, her bedroll jouncing on her hip, pain tweaking at her right arm.

She was too late. Ian was already halfway across the patch and floundering. "It's awful soft. Look, my feet are going right in."

"Come back. Quick."

Ian tried to turn, staggered, and fell to his knees. As his hands went forward to save himself, they sank into the sand up to the elbows. As he struggled to free himself, screaming with panic now, his legs were driven deeper under the surface.

"Stop struggling like that, Ian! Now listen. Can you get your bedroll off your shoulder? Come on. You can do it. That's right. Now push it in front of you and hold on to it, lying as flat as you can."

"Megan, I'm going under!"

"No, you're not, silly billy. Just listen and you'll be all right. You've got to kick with your legs, like you were swimming."

"But I can't swim."

"Just kick. Kind of slow. And try to wriggle forward on the bedroll."

As she talked Megan was tossing her canteen aside, slipping her bedroll off her shoulder. She ran toward Ian, felt the subtle difference in the quality of the sand. Shifting, insecure. She drew back quickly as it pulled at the soles of her shoes.

Ian was now lying flat, the front of his thighs and calves under the sand. He'd managed to get his arms free all right, and they were stretched out in front of him, clutching the bedroll. His kicking was getting him nowhere, though. Each time he moved, his knees bent and drove him a little farther under the sand.

"Meg!" His eyes were squeezed shut, and the knuckles of the hands clutching the bedroll were white.

She stood frozen, unable to think, unable to do anything.

He's going to get tired and he'll panic and struggle some more. Sooner or later the rest of his body's going to go under. Are you going to stand here and watch him die?

She heard Mom's voice in her head. *Look after Ian, Meg love. Promise?*

I promise, Mom.

But I don't know what to do. Oh, Mom, help me! I can't . . .

Yes, you do. The voice was calm. *Keep your head. You can use the rope around your bedroll to reach him.*

The rope! Of course! Megan dropped to her knees. Her stiff fingers fumbled with the knots that fastened the rope around her blanket. Come on. There. At last it was free.

She tied one end to the belt strap of her jeans and stood up to throw the other end toward Ian. It fell short by maybe a yard. The rest lay loose on the sand. There was plenty of length. Just not enough weight.

Ian saw the end of rope and tried to struggle toward it. She saw the heels of his worn canvas shoes vanish beneath the sand. "No! Don't move!" she screamed and pulled the rope back.

Weight. That's what was needed. A stone, maybe. Her eyes darted from side to side, rejecting this pebble as too small, that stone as too smooth. At last, there. The perfect shape, long enough so she could snug a slip knot around its middle without its falling right off again.

"Ian, I'm going to throw it so it lands close to your head. Keep your face down against your bedroll. Don't grab it. Don't move at all. And—and don't worry if I have to take a couple of tries at it."

Megan made sure that the rope was lying loose on the ground, not touching anything that could snag it. Without thinking, she took the stone, with the end of the rope tied around it, in her right hand and threw. It fell far short, over to Ian's right, and the pain that shot down her arm reminded her why. Stupid! Use your left arm.

This was harder. The stone didn't want to leave her hand and her arm felt clumsy. Come on. You can do it. You've got to.

She gritted her teeth, drew her arm back, aimed, and threw. The stone hurled through the air, the rope snaking after it, and landed neatly on the bedroll to the left of Ian's head.

Megan wiped her hands across her face and licked her dry lips. "Okay, Ian." She tried to keep the panic out of her voice. "Just move your left hand. Nothing else. Pull the rope toward you and undo the slip knot. Can you manage?"

She couldn't see. The air between them shimmered with heat. She rubbed her hand over her blurring eyes.

"Yeah. What do I do now, Meg?"

"Push the end of the rope through the strap of your bedroll. Get a good end through. *Don't move the rest of you, Ian!*"

"I'm sorry. I forgot." He was on the edge of tears. "I've got the rope through."

"Now you've got to tie a bowline."

"I don't know—"

"Yes, you do. I taught you, back on the farm."

"I don't remember." His voice went up, only a small step away from hysteria.

Megan squatted at the edge of the sand river. "Sure you do. I'll help you. It'll be okay. You start by twisting the far end of the rope into a gopher hole—"

"Yeah!"

"Now remember, the loose end of rope's the gopher. He comes out of his hole, runs around the rope—"

"And he sees me and runs back in again." Ian's voice was triumphant.

"Atta boy! You've done it. Now just give the rope a little tug, just to make sure you've done it right. Try not to move the rest of you."

"It's okay, Meg. I done it right."

"Good boy. Now hang on to your bedroll with both arms and don't let go. Keep your head down. I'm going to pull you out."

She stood up again, wrapped the rope twice around

her hands, and walked slowly backward until it was taut.

Dear God, please let him have done the bowline right. Please.

She leaned back. Fine sand flew from the rope as it twanged tight.

And please let the rope be okay. Not rotten, all right? she added hastily.

She put all her weight against the load at the other end of the rope. Neither the bedroll nor Ian's body budged. The rope creaked alarmingly and Megan's hands swelled and reddened against the tightened coils around them. She took an extra twist and leaned back again, her heels digging into the sandy dirt.

Was that a movement? Or was it the knot slipping?

"Ian, try and kick your legs just a little. Sideways, not up and down. Like a frog swimming. Remember how a frog swims? But don't let go with your arms."

He *was* moving. She could see the whitish glint of the heels of his canvas shoes. She leaned back, the sweat pouring down her face and neck. Now she could see the backs of his calves. The backs of his thighs.

"Now straighten your legs and lie real flat, like you're a board," she yelled and took a good step back. And another . . .

Now he was scooting across the top of the sand

toward her, leaving a ridge of sand like a wave on either side. Then the bedroll hit the edge of solid ground and she felt the jar right up her arms into her shoulders. She loosened the rope from her hands and pulled him over the top of the bedroll to safety. And she was sitting on the ground with her arms around him, holding him, rocking him.

"Meg, I can't breathe."

She let him go and sat back. He stared. "What are you crying for? It's okay."

"I am?" She scrubbed her face on the sleeve of her cotton shirt and managed a shaky laugh. "Guess I'm just glad to see your ugly face again."

"Me too," Ian said cheekily and scrambled to his feet. Now that the danger was past it was as if it had never happened. "Can you believe it? You can't tell by looking at all." He walked over to the edge of the unstable sand.

"You just get back from there, Ian Dougal, or I'll have your hide."

Even looking at the smoothly innocent sand gave Megan the horrors. How had it happened? Perhaps, long ago, there had been a gully here that had filled up with fine sand to make a death trap for the unwary. Death by drowning . . . in a gully full of sand!

She shivered and couldn't stop shivering in spite of

the heat. She envied Ian his ability to forget what had happened and live in the present. For the rest of that day the nightmare of *what if* kept coming back to haunt her. She refused to let Ian run ahead, but bundled all their possessions into the one big roll, using the freed rope as a safety line, fastened about each of their waists. She mourned the loss of her lucky crystal.

Though Mitch's sketch map told them to go west, the sand river was like an invisible barrier between them and the all-weather road that should lie on the far side. Twice Megan ventured onto a patch of smooth stone-free sand, only to feel it shift beneath her feet.

By the time the sun was dropping behind the Rockies, she was getting worried. Before long it would be dark. And in the dark it would be impossible to tell firm sand from shifting until it was too late. She didn't like the idea of spending the night out here on the open empty plain. There were no buildings. Nothing they could use for firewood.

And the coyotes were prowling. Like an echo to her fear she heard the long drawn-out howl. And an answer. And another. They sounded much louder than they had on previous nights.

"They've been close by." Ian broke the eerie silence.

"What?"

"Them coyotes. They've been here."

"How d'you know?"

"Footprints. Look." He pointed at the ground ahead of them.

The footprints ran from left to right. Megan's eyes followed the tracks to the west. They ran across the smoothness of the sand river.

"I wonder how much coyotes weigh?"

"As much as me?"

"I don't think so. Maybe half. The prints don't sink in that deep, do they?"

"There's tufts of grass growing out there, Meg."

"Maybe I could get across to them. You wait here and hang on to your end of the rope. It's worth a try." Meg slipped the weight of the doubled bedroll from her shoulder with a sigh of relief. "Hang on, then."

She stepped onto the smooth fine sand and took a step forward. The sand shivered uneasily under her weight. She could feel her shoes sinking and began to panic. But the coyotes had managed. Their stride was long, she noticed. I bet they didn't stand around worrying, she told herself, and forced her legs to carry her as lightly and quickly as they could to the safety of the grass tussock.

"It's okay so far. Can you make it over here with both bedrolls, Ian?"

"Sure. Nothing to it." He ran to her, unafraid.

She looked at the next stretch. "Okay, Ian. Here I

go." She ran with despair in her heart, feeling her feet slip uneasily. It was as if she were running across a bowl of mush. She tripped, felt her heart jump with fright, and landed on all fours on pebbles that dug into hands and knees.

She sat up, laughing, licking the grazes on her palms. "It's all right, Ian! We're across!"

Shortly afterward, the road appeared beneath their feet without warning, and they turned south and followed it until it was almost too dark to see. Where it turned west again there was an abandoned shed close to the road. They kicked the planks loose and broke them up for a fire.

"But there's not enough of anything growing to start a grass fire," Ian objected when Megan made him haul the wood to the fence and over onto the road surface.

"Better safe than sorry." That was one of Mom's phrases, wasn't it?

"Yes, ma'am." Ian grinned cheekily, and Megan felt her heart squeeze so tight she could hardly breathe at the thought of how easily he might have been lying under a couple of yards of sand instead of running around sassing her.

Now that the immediate danger was over, she was beginning to feel very peculiar indeed. Her arm ached savagely. That was to be expected. She hoped she hadn't done any permanent damage. It didn't seem to have started bleeding again. But it was the shaky feeling in her stomach, the sense that at any minute she might burst into uncontrollable tears, that made her move cautiously, talk as little as possible, even stop looking at Ian—because behind his chubby face and pink cheeks, she could see the face of death grinning at her.

Silently she fed the fire, so that the coals glowed red and sparks flew up into the still air to join the stars that were beginning to show in the darkening sky. But the fire also brought shadows, and twilight became dark night.

Megan shivered and busied herself unwrapping the food that Sadie had given them, kept fresh in an old dish towel. There was a chicken, already roasted. No need to wait for it to cook. Just cut off the legs and sit close to the comforting light and eat till her trembly stomach was full. There was bread, too, delicious toasted over the hot coals. And fresh water.

By the time they had finished their silent meal, Ian was nodding.

"Bedtime."

"Megan, are you still mad at me?"

"Mad? Of course not. What made you . . ."

"'Cause you've not said a word all evening. I'm sorry. I didn't mean to fall in the sand."

"Oh, Ian." Megan put her arms around him. "It's

okay. And of course I'm not mad. Just . . . I guess I'm tired."

But long after Ian was asleep, Megan lay staring into the last embers of the fire. The howls of the coyotes seemed very near. She shivered and put another piece of wood on the fire.

NINE

I t was a horrible dream. She and Ian were up to their necks in sand. She could move her head and her eyes. Nothing more. And out there, beyond the circle of their sandy prison, something was watching them. She opened her mouth to yell. "Help," "Help," came mocking cries from the darkness. It turned into the howling of guard dogs and she made an enormous effort to break free of the trap.

She sat up suddenly, her blanket falling away from her shoulders. A shadow between her and the fire suddenly faded away into the darkness. She blinked and clutched her blanket. Had she really seen anything? Or was it just the dregs of her dream?

She reached out and pushed a long piece of tinder-dry wood into the embers, stirring them up. The dry wood flared and she held it above her head like a torch. Red eyes shone and vanished.

Two pairs? Three? Four?

Behind her something rustled. She jumped to her feet and whirled around in time to see another elusive shadow blend into the darkness. Her heart thumped against her chest. She reached down quickly to pull the remaining wood close to the fire, her eyes on the twin red shapes, like coals glowing in the dark, a reflection of her own fire. She dumped all the wood on at once. For an instant it was dark and she thought: stupid, I should have been more careful. Now it's out and we're alone in the dark with these beasts.

But it was all right. A cheerful crackling broke the sinister silence and there was an explosion of light, making a safe magic circle around the fire. Within it they were safe. Beyond were flickering light and shadows. Beyond that, the darkest dark. Where was the moon? Had it not risen yet? Or perhaps it had already set. How long had she been asleep?

She looked down at Ian, curled under his blanket, the firelight dancing off the pinky-blond of his hair. I'd kill for him, she thought. I'd die for him. Not just because of the promise to Mom. But for *him*.

◆

The dry wood was burning fast in the blaze. There was no more. She'd used every last splinter. No way was she going to leave Ian sleeping while she went for more. Suppose . . .

"Hey, wake up." She bent over and shook his shoulders gently. "Wake up, Ian!"

"Wha . . .? Is it morning already?" He gave a huge yawn and sat up, tousle-headed, blinking like an owl.

Megan explained. "Stay close to the fire and keep your eyes open," she finished. "If any of those darn coyotes come close, just grab a piece of wood out of the fire and poke it at them. You'll be okay."

"What about you, Meg? It's dark out there."

"I'll take this." Megan held up her torch, now with only a glow at its charred tip. She blew at it until sparks flew and flames suddenly flared from it. "I'll be all right. It isn't far." She was reassuring herself as much as Ian.

Getting over the barbed-wire fence with the torch in one hand was the real nuisance. She ran toward the ruined shed, a dark shape in the darkness, imagining coyote teeth nipping at her heels. She kicked viciously at the remains, bringing them down in a cloud of acrid dust that made her cough. Only one hand. The other had to hold the torch. It was her only protection. She caught together all the splintered wood she could manage in her left arm.

Watch out for rusty nails. That was one of Mom's warnings. Like: *Always wear a hat in the sun* and *Brush your teeth after meals.*

Sorry, Mom. There's no time to worry about all that. I'll just have to hope I don't get scratched. I guess I'm likelier to get chewed up by a bunch of starving coyotes than to get sick from a rusty nail.

She whirled the torch about over her head to revive the dying flame and plodded back to the fence with her load.

"Ian, you there?"

"Yeah. Hand it over." He appeared in the darkness by the fence.

"Watch out for rusty nails," she found herself saying in Mom's voice.

"Yes, ma'am." He was making fun of her again, but it didn't make her mad anymore. They were on the same side now and teasing didn't hurt.

By the time she'd climbed the fence, Ian had already built up the fire. They saw no more shadowy figures, no more red eyes gleaming in the light of the fire. From far over in the west came a long yarping wail. Then another. And another. In the sound was wrapped up all the sadness and hunger and the awful loneliness of the spoiled country.

Megan shivered and crouched close to the fire. She thrust another piece of wood into its heart. The flames rose, blotting out the stars. They sat close together, blankets around their shoulders.

"D'you think they'll be back?" Ian gave a jaw-cracking yawn.

"Guess not. Listen. They're way off now. Looking for another kind of dinner."

The fire died down and the shape of the country began to remake itself out of darkness. Not long till dawn, Megan guessed. She could see the eastern horizon clearly against the line of the land.

"What's that?" Ian pointed south.

In a way the lights were like coyote eyes. First one pair. Then another. Gleaming. Then vanishing. They can't be animals—too far off, Megan puzzled. And animals' eyes only shine in the reflection of another light, like our fire.

"Why, they must be lights of cars. And that'll be the highway west."

"Looky, Meg. Four. Five. Six."

"That's the lot."

"Where d'you suppose they're going?"

"Through the mountains. On to the Kootenays,

maybe. Or right through to the coast. Look, Ian, here comes another bunch."

"Tell me again what a car's like, Meg."

She rubbed her hand thoughtfully over her nose. "Like a metal box on wheels, 'bout the size of the kitchen table, I guess. Inside two sets of seats. Like two sofas one behind the other."

"I know that. I've seen pictures in *The World Book*. But what are they really like?"

"I don't remember being in a car. But the school bus—it was hot and it smelled kind of funny. Oil and hot metal and gas. And real noisy. On the dirt roads it jumped around a lot and we all bumped into each other. We used to sing. It was fun."

"D'you suppose they're singing, over there?"

"Maybe."

"Why are the cars all bunched up like that? Four or five? Then a gap, and another lot?"

Megan thought about it. "I guess they travel at night because it's cooler. And all together because . . . maybe because they're scared."

"Scared of what?"

"All this. The darkness. The emptiness. Us."

"Us?" Ian giggled.

"I expect so."

They watched the distant road. There were no more

headlights. The fire died down to gray ash and embers. The howls of the coyotes were a very long way off, remote and unthreatening. Megan wondered if the people in the cars could hear them above the noises of their engines. What would they do? Roll up the windows, she imagined, and drive on, holding the steering wheels tight, tight.

"Come on, let's get a bit more sleep, shall we? It's too dark to walk yet."

They snuggled into their blankets.

"Meg?" Ian's voice came sleepily out of the darkness.

"Hmm?"

"They're scared of this place? Of us?"

"Yeah, I guess so."

"Then we're smarter than they are, aren't we? We know how to live here."

"You'd better believe it. Now go to sleep."

◆

They woke as the sun rose, to a day that in some strange way smelled fresher. As if they'd left the dry land behind them.

They breakfasted on barley bread, goat cheese, and the last of the chicken, and then they set out at a good pace along the road that led west, the land slowly falling away to their left. Now, perhaps a mile away, was a dark line of scrub.

Megan consulted her map. "The Crowsnest River. Ian, we're almost there!"

Their road turned to meet the river and soon they were following it, close by, but high above, as the river twisted through a deeply cut channel in the rock.

The river was in fact several rivers, braided together, with banks of sand and pebbles and even small tree-covered islands between the braids. It was good to leave the wasteland behind them. Now there was the green of chokecherry and saskatoon and the silvery green of wolf willow growing down in the valley, while up at the level of the road, grasses were struggling to establish themselves again.

Megan strode along, barely aware of the pebbles against the thin soles of her canvas shoes or the monotonous ache in her right arm. They were heading the right way. By day's end they should have reached the waterfall. All she had to do was to find Uncle Greg and she would have kept her promise to Mom. Ian would be safe.

He too was in good spirits this morning. "That's the highway over there, I bet. D'you see it, Meg? I hope I get to see a car. D'you think I'll get to see a car soon, Meg?"

The sun was well up in the southeastern sky by the time they reached a crossroads. A battered sign, pockmarked with buckshot and rust, said TO HIGHWAY 3.

"You mean we're going to cross the highway? What'll we do if we see a car coming? Suppose . . ."

"I bet we don't. But we'll be careful, don't worry."

A metal bridge took them high over the river. They hung over the railing and watched the water slide beneath. There was not a lot of it.

"Shall we go down and fill the canteens?" Ian asked.

Megan shook her head. "There's a trail down there, must lead to a house. I don't think we'll risk it. We'll stick with Mitch's map. There's enough water to last the day. Come on."

After the bridge the road led them southwest up to the highway. It was wide and paved with black stuff, but frost-heaves and potholes had eaten away at the surface, and weeds had made a home in the eaten-away places. It was empty to right and left as far as they could see.

Together they ran across its width, exclaiming as the hardtop burned the thin soles of their shoes. Beyond the highway the country was stony, with hills rising to the south, hills that were covered with trees, scrubby pines as well as the slender stems of aspen.

The road led them southward into a new kind of country. They could no longer see clearly to a distant horizon. On every side they were surrounded by small hills. There was no knowing what might lie beyond the next bend or behind the next rock or tree trunk.

By the time they came to the old highway, it was high noon and the shimmer of heat on the hardtop was unbearable. They backed off the road into the brush and found a spot between rocks, tree shaded, the earth soft and smelling sweetly of pine needles. Here they slept through the afternoon.

When Ian woke, Megan was consulting the map, smoothing the grubby piece of paper out on her knee.

"Where've we got to?"

"Right here. We've just got to go one, maybe two miles along this old road—Highway 3A, Mitch calls it. Says it's closed, so we don't have to worry about cars going by. And there, at the end, see? That's the falls. Same as the picture on the calendar in the kitchen back home. D'you remember, Ian? That's where we're going to find Uncle Greg."

He didn't say anything. She folded up the map and jumped to her feet. "So c'mon. Let's get going. Now." She slung the heavy bedroll over her shoulder. "So come on, slowpoke. What's holding you up?"

"Nothin'." Ian followed her slowly through the trees up to the road. "Meg, suppose Uncle Greg's not there. What'll we do? Will we go back to Mitch's?"

"He'll be there." *He's got to be there.*

The hardtop was taffy soft in the sun, its heat burning their feet. They tried walking along the edge of the road, but it was stony and uneven. Ian strayed away, up a slope to their left.

"Looky over here, Meg. See what I found."

Meg found him balancing on a shiny steel rail. "That must be the railway line. Where the trains go by. No, Ian, you can't possibly walk the rail. You'll just slip off and twist your ankle and then where'll we be? But along the middle here, on the wooden crosspieces, it's not bad. And cooler than that old highway down there, that's for sure."

They walked along the ties, which had the magic smell of the pine trees. The hill on their left cast its shadow over the line. The rails ran for the most part straight and shiny toward the falls, like a dream road leading them on.

Suddenly Ian, who'd decided to try balancing on the rail again, jumped off. "Meg!" His face was scared. "Meg, the earth's shaking."

"It can't be, silly. I don't feel—" She stopped and bent to touch the rail, felt the tremor running up her arm. "What? Oh, Ian, it's a train coming. Get off the line, quick!"

She dragged him off the rail and down the slope of the right-of-way. They fell to the ground among the grass and weeds.

The vibration was now a sound, now a roar like

thunder, a shaking of the whole world. They could feel it in the ground under them. Pebbles whirled down from the rails. Dust filled the air. Then a shrieking monster flew past them, dragging boxcar after boxcar. Rocking. Roaring. Clacking over the rails. Megan flung her arm across Ian and buried her face in his shoulders.

Then it was gone. The dust settled. Silence rushed into the heat of the afternoon. A squirrel among the pine trees began to chatter and scold.

"What was it?"

"A train. I'd forgotten trains."

"Let's not walk on the line anymore, Meg, okay?"

"Okay." She managed a shaky laugh. "We'll stick to the road, even if it is hot."

They plodded on. Sometimes they walked in shadow. Sometimes the sun beat down on their heads and shoulders.

"Boy, it's a long way."

"Look up ahead, Ian."

"I don't see nothin."

"It's a bridge. A bridge back across the river. That's where Mitch's map ends. That's the falls!"

She dropped her bedroll and ran along the hot road, her feet pounding against the tacky hardtop. She ran until a stitch knifed her side and still she ran on, until she was brought up short by the barrier of a rusted chain-metal fence, her hands grasping the top.

Directly ahead was the Crowsnest River, a gentle stream split by a stony island. Her eyes followed the river. It came to a craggy edge and fell, down into a deeply gouged ravine some fifty or sixty feet deep that lay directly, giddily below her. The water fell in silvery ropes and threads, like necklaces of white, foaming at the bottom, a little mist rising, catching the sun. . . .

"That's not a bit like the calendar back home." Ian's voice was disgusted. "It's just a bitty trickle. You mean we come all this way for *that*, Megan Dougal?"

"D'you see those plants growing halfway up in the rock? See how green they are. And look. The spray's making tiny rainbows."

"But it isn't—"

She turned on him. "D'you expect it to look just like the picture? That was thirteen years ago, for pete's sake. And it was probably an old photo then."

"Well, don't get mad at me, Megan Dougal. It's not my fault. And why're you crying? You can't fool me. You expected the falls to be just like they was in the picture, didn't you, huh?"

"It's been a dry summer. You should see it in the spring just after the snow's melted."

They both jumped at the strange voice and Megan gulped back a scream. They had been arguing so loudly they'd never heard the stranger's feet on the stony ground.

Megan's hand went out automatically in a peaceful gesture, palms open. Her eyes darted around. He was alone. No dogs. No guns. Only then did she really look at the stranger's face. Her hands dropped and she smiled.

He was about sixteen years old, his hair under the brim of his hat brown and wavy, growing down to his shoulders, his eyes hazel with a darker rim. When he smiled his teeth were very white. He smelled clean and his clothes, a simple long-sleeved shirt of homespun over loosely cut pants, were freshly laundered.

Megan suddenly became uncomfortably aware that she was standing very close to the stranger, that she was staring at him, and worse still, that she smelled, that her clothes were travel-stained, and she hadn't brushed her teeth or her hair since they'd left Sadie's.

She tried to back off and hit the fence. His hand shot out and grasped her arm, steadying her, pulling her forward, toward him. "I wouldn't lean on that fence if I were you. It's pretty old, and the ground at the edge gives way once in a while. It'd be a pity to end up at the bottom of the river. So who are you? Where are you from? And where are you heading?"

"I'm Megan Dougal and this here's my brother, Ian. We used to have a poultry farm close by Fort Macleod, but then our mom died, and—" Megan stopped, brought up short suddenly by the possibility of rejection. Suppose Uncle Greg wasn't around anymore? Suppose this young man—she didn't even know his name—suppose he and his family and friends wanted nothing to do with a pair of scruffy travel-worn kids? Suppose . . . ?

"I guess you're on your way out west, then. Most everyone is. You've missed the road, though. You need to cross the bridge and follow the old road west." His hand on her shoulder turned her gently around. He pointed. "It connects up with the Crowsnest Trail again and you should be able to get a lift from there."

"But we don't want to—" Megan began.

"We're planning on staying *here*," Ian blurted out at the same time.

The friendly smile had gone, as if someone had turned off a light inside the stranger's head. "Here? I'm sorry, but—"

"Uncle Greg. He used to live here. I guess it's here." Megan looked around at the falls, the bridge, the fence. The road running by. There wasn't a house in sight.

"You said your name was Dougal, didn't you? There's no one of that name here."

"Not Dougal. Uncle Greg's my *mom's* brother."

Megan racked her brain for the name. Stupid. How stupid not to remember what Mom was called before she was married. It had been in the family Bible, she remembered that. Births, marriages, and deaths, on the pages between the contents and Genesis. She'd looked so as to get Mom's name when they'd buried her and the baby. Rosemary. Rosemary something . . .

"McKinnon. Rosemary McKinnon. That was her name."

Coolness was replaced by a kind of respect on the boy's face. She found her knees were trembling.

"It's all right, then? He's still alive? He's here?"

"Sure is." The boy grinned. "I'll take you to his house."

"Oh, my bedroll. I dropped the bundle somewhere...." Megan looked around vaguely.

"You sure did. And your canteen." Ian handed them over with a righteous look.

"I'll carry it. You look beat. How about you, kid? Why don't you let me give you a hand with your load?"

"I'm fine. I can manage." Ian flushed up at being called "kid" and hitched his load over his shoulder with a defiant look at the older boy. Megan gave him a smile and a nod. I'll tell them all later how great he was, how he saved my life.

Right now she had to half run to keep even with the boy as he led the way south of the river toward a small thicket of aspen. The ground was still sandy here, she noticed, but with a lot more texture to it than the country through which they had just traveled. In places shaly rock broke through the surface. In others there were pockets of richer dirt, where brush, flowering plants, and trees flourished.

There was no path and she had to pick her way between the bushes, which caught at her hair and clothes. Then, unexpectedly, they were in a clearing and ahead of them lay a well-defined path leading westward. On their left the hillside was covered with aspen and evergreen. To their right she caught glimpses of the river between the bushes. It meandered peacefully along, as if it didn't know its destiny was over the falls.

She turned back. The thicket hid them completely from the road and the railway.

"Yes." He answered her unspoken question. "The path used to run straight through. We let it grow over to discourage strangers."

Us? she thought, but his smile took the edge off his remark. "If you've traveled far you'll know the kind of people I mean. There's still bad folks around, though not so many as there used to be a few years ago. We've got something worth protecting here. You'll see."

As the trail led them uphill, Megan caught a glimpse of a log house, gray among the trees. And then, across the road, another. Small paths wound upward into the hills. A bird sang shrilly from the shadow of a thicket. It was almost cool under the trees.

Then, quite unexpectedly, the trail curved to the right. The hills fell away behind them. Ahead was a great upland meadow and beyond it the sweep of the Rockies. The land was carefully contoured and cultivated, the plots edged with stone-lined culverts that led back to where the hills rose behind her.

She saw the small details of cultivation, but was too full of unexpected emotions to ask about them. She didn't have any words. A lark was singing passionately overhead. The wind blew sweetly out of the mountains. The air was sparklingly fresh. She felt a joyfulness that hurt inside her. And a pain as she thought—if only Mom were here.

"Master Greg's house is just over the rise here." The boy turned and took her arm, urging her forward. She tried to keep up, limping in her worn canvas shoes. As the ground fell away they saw ahead and below them the roof of another log house, facing west, toward the mountains. The boy dropped her arm and ran ahead, calling out, "Master Gregory! You'll never guess who's here!"

Megan and Ian followed him down, around the house to the front porch. As they arrived a big man came out, a man with a beard and wiry hair the texture of Megan's own unmanageable hair. He came closer and she saw that he had Mom's eyes.

When he saw them he gave a great shout and held his

arms wide. Ian dropped his load and ran straight into them, while Megan stood, suddenly shy, until his arm came out and gathered her in.

"Rosemary's daughter! I'd have known you anywhere even without Gideon here naming you for me."

From the safe circle of his arm Megan looked out at the boy, now also named, no longer a stranger. Gideon, she thought. Yes. Then she felt the warmth of her uncle's body, she could lean her tiredness against his strength and look at Ian, safely clasped in his other arm. They'd done it!

TEN

The rafters of the great log house were hung with evergreens and berries, and the tables of the community hall were laden with roast chickens, potatoes, carrots, turnips, pies, and puddings. At the crowded tables, everyone was wearing their festive best.

As Megan looked around the room, her eyes resting on familiar smiling faces, the faces of her friends and neighbors in the community of Gaia, she got a sudden flashback to their first meeting. It had taken place in this very hall, the day after their arrival and their welcome by Gideon and Uncle Greg. That night she had taken for granted that they would be equally welcomed by the rest of the community, but she had been wrong. "We're a community, Gregory, and it should be a community decision," a thin-faced man called Tim Freuchen had said.

"Aye, there's none of us has sent for relatives to come here and live soft after all the real work's been done." This was a large woman with bright red hair, her name Joanne Turpin.

"That's not fair, Joanne," protested John Weyburn, a gentle-voiced man. "Greg didn't send for them. They come on their own, like orphans in need. Are we that mean and ingrown we'd turn away orphans? We're no better than survivalists, if that's so."

"That's soft thinking, John. Listen, all of you. We've worked desperate hard for the last eleven years. We've gentled the soil and healed some of Earth's wounds. Now she's repaying us with crops enough to live on. But that's because we stay small. We don't crowd the land or pollute the water or wear out the soil."

"We all know that. What's it got to do with—"

"Once we start letting in outsiders there'll be no end to it. We voted on that once before, don't you remember? When we closed the road into the community."

"D'you really think that Gaia is so fragile that two extra children will be the ruin of it, Tim?" Uncle Greg had smiled as he spoke, Megan noticed, but his eyes didn't smile. She wondered then, with a sickening drop in her stomach, what she and Ian would do if they weren't allowed to stay.

I am so very tired, she had thought, and desperately tried to blink back the tears that were threatening to pour out of her eyes. Then the obstinacy that had carried her through the death of Mom and the baby, through dragging the reluctant Ian over miles of parched prairie and foothills in spite of dogs and guns and quicksand, surged up again.

She had stood up in front of the roomful of strangers, flushed with embarrassment but determined to have her say. "We came here 'cause Uncle Greg's our only kin. Before Mom died she told us about him and about the community he started out here. We came on our own, just the two of us. We met some bad people and some crazy ones. We got hurt, but we kept going. We'd only gophers and weeds to eat, but we came through. So you know we're not soft. I know we're just a couple of kids, but we'll work to pay you back for our food and clothing if you let us stay.

"As for what you believe in, well, we sure understand that, Ian and me. We met a Peigan man, Mike Spotted Eagle was his name. He and his friends were living in an old museum at the buffalo jump. He was a bit crazy, but not all that crazy. He told me how they'd used that buffalo jump for thousands of years, before the pyramids and a place called Stonehenge was built. How they'd respected the land. Then the white people had come out of the east, kind of blinding them with words, I guess, and they'd grabbed the land and cut it into squares. They'd drained the swamps and dammed the rivers, just to get more and more out of the land.

"Then there was Mitch and Sadie. They were good people. They told us about how thousands of years ago, people turned a fertile land into a desert, just 'cause they got greedy. And that's what's happening now. So we know what Gaia's about. Now if you decide you don't want us, then thank you kindly for the night's shelter and food, and we'll be on our way."

♦

Now here they all were, in the same great log house in the community of Gaia, two years later, Thanksgiving day, Monday, October 14, 2013.

"What are you grinning at?" Ian leaned across the table to ask.

"I was remembering that first day, with everyone sitting around judging whether they'd let us stay."

"And you sure told them where to go! I thought you'd gone crazy. I was in a panic that they'd take you up on it and then where'd we have been?"

Megan chuckled. "Telling them we'd walk clear through the Rockies to Peachland and find Mitch and Sadie's son was what decided them, I think."

"Boy, you sure were mad that day!"

She looked at Ian—surrounded by his friends, already taller than she was, with real muscles—and tears prickled her eyes. She closed them, remembering. The lonely grave in the sand-filled irrigation canal. The Peigan man. The survivalists with their dogs and guns. Dear Sadie and Mitch, without whom they'd have surely died; two years later, still farming their beloved patch of land, but now someone from the Gaia community rode out once in a while to see if they needed anything—and came back the richer for Sadie's baking. Oh, Mom, Megan thought. I wish you could see Ian right now. You'd be real proud. I did all right, didn't I?

She blinked and her hand went automatically to her throat, feeling the water-smoothed jade stone that hung there, found and given to her by Gideon on her last birthday. It didn't exactly replace the lost crystal drop. That had been like a promise of water, driving her on. But she and Ian had arrived. She didn't need the crystal drop anymore. And there was another kind of promise in the smooth green stone.

Then Uncle Greg thumped the table for attention and stood up, glass of chokecherry wine in hand. "Friends.

Companions of Gaia. In 1578 Martin Frobisher and his fellow explorers celebrated the first North American Thanksgiving up in the barrens of the eastern Arctic. Since that time we have come together at different times and in different ways to give thanks to Almighty God for the bountiful harvest with which our land has been blessed. Those are the words that came to be used. But for a long time past Thanksgiving has been a bitter day for a lot of farmers. For decades we'd forgotten that giving is a two-way street. We took and took until the poor land was clean worn out, with nothing more to give but dust and winds.

"But, thank God, we've been given a second chance. There's not a lot us country folk can do about the ozone layer and the greenhouse effect that we haven't already done or been forced to do by circumstance. We've had to give up cattle and chemical fertilizers. We burn as little wood as we can and rely on wind and solar power for our needs. For the rest, well, it's up to our world governments to come to their senses. We do what we can. *Gaia* is the word for the life-force of Earth, which will restore our planet, if we give her half a chance. So, on the fourteenth Thanksgiving since the founding of our community, I give you a toast. Earth, God bless her."

They stood to drink the toast together, and sat to

eat their way through the banquet. Voices rose and laughter.

"I've something to tell you, Megan." Gideon spoke so softly that she had to lean against his shoulder to hear. "They've accepted me at Western Desert College. Me and Mike Freuchen."

"In Kamloops? Oh, Gid, when do you have to go?"

"Right away, now all the crops are dug. We'll start out tomorrow. Not sure when we'll get there. Only a day if we're lucky hitching a ride, but there aren't that many cars going through anymore."

"What'll you learn there that Uncle Greg hasn't already taught you? He's the expert on Gaia."

"He says he's fifteen years out of date. Sure, we know how to contour the hills and have stone-lined paths leading the rain down to our fields. We've got trickle-irrigation and we've learned a lot of ways to conserve moisture. But he says that college can teach us a whole lot more. There are new hybrid crops for the new climate conditions. Different trees and ground cover. Maybe new techniques in solar power."

"We're doing all right now."

"Sure we are. But we should move out and teach other groups. And the colony's going to grow, as our generation marries and has kids. There's got to be enough to support them too. And that's what I want to ask you, Megan. I'll be gone two years. Will you wait for me? Maybe marry me when I get back?"

Megan looked around the crowded hall, at the laughing faces of her friends, her family, joking, waving chicken legs for emphasis. The noise rose. What a time and place for a proposal! But then, what better?

"Wait for you, Gideon?" She drew herself up and stuck out her chin obstinately. "Next year I'll have finished school. I'm going to get such good marks they'll send me to college too. Will *you* wait for *me*?"

ABOUT THE AUTHOR

Monica Hughes has won many prizes for her writing, including the Canada Council Prize for Children's Literature, which she received twice, and a Certificate of Honor from the International Board on Books for Young People for *Keeper of the Isis Light,* which was also an American Library Association Best Book for Young Adults. Her other titles include *Hunter in the Dark,* also an ALA Best Book for Young Adults; *Sandwriter; Invitation to the Game;* and *The Promise.*

Monica Hughes lives in Canada.